I0570825

# LIFESTYLE

A Tale of Upscale Suburbia and a Girl

## SIMON PLASTER

Copyright © 2012 by Simon Plaster

All rights reserved.  Published by Mossik Press

mossikpress@mail.com

Library of Congress Cataloging-in-Publication Data

Plaster, Simon [11.15.2012]

Lifestyle: A Tale of Upscale Suburbia and a Girl
by Simon Plaster

p.  cm.

ISBN 978-0-615-72331-0

1. Mystery—Fiction.
2. Oklahoma, United States—Fiction.
3. Suburban Living—Fiction.

10 9 8 7 6 5 4 3 2 1

LIFESTYLE is entirely a work of satirical fiction and in no way an account or reference to actual persons, places, institutions and events — past, present or predicted. Any suggestion to the contrary is strictly unintended and coincidental.

—SP/MP

# LIFESTYLE

A Tale of Upscale Suburbia and a Girl

## SIMON PLASTER

MOSSIK PRESS

# CHELMSFORD HEIGHTS WOMEN'S ALLIANCE
for
Upscale Lifestyle, Liberty and Pursuit of Happiness

---

Mr. Harold Mixon
Editor & Publisher
*Weekly Weekender*
Chelmsford Heights, OK

Dear Sir:

Regrettably, I must again express my extreme displeasure with *Weekender* reportage of community affairs since your acquisition of our local newspaper — this time with reference to last weekend's front page article, headlined HORSES' ASHES HONORED AT CEREMONY. In fact, at dedication of the new John "Jack" Johnson Columbarium Wing of the Chelmsford Heights Hall of Fame, the cremated remains of Mrs. Johnson's beloved show mare ("Jilly")and ashes of her late beloved mate ("Mister Jack") were <u>not</u> inurned! They were mixed with a sack of cement to make the miniature statue which Mrs. Johnson was shown mounted upon.

More to the point, totally garbled in your article, Mason jars containing the cremated remains of two dozen other prominent past residents of Chelmsford Heights <u>were</u> placed in Columbarium niches after raw remains were <u>disinterred</u> from their former location that need not have been disclosed. Your crude reference to them having been "dug up"—coupled with the very unfortunate content and placement of a wholly unrelated photograph—was unforgivably tasteless. Under your editorial stewardship, must we now be <u>shown</u>, of all ghastly things, sewer line repairs in progress?! Are we to display upon our coffee tables pictures of ourselves in the company of those of shirtless, overweight men in obscenely drooping trousers, digging in a ditch filled—one can only hope—with muddy rain water? We devoutly demand <u>not</u>!

And Mr. Mixon, in the strongest of terms I must caution you—an unknitted newcomer to our close-knit community—<u>do not</u> rake the muck in which we have buried and put out of our minds the past misfortunes of our Founding Family, the Grossmans. Grandfather Leo, though having reached the forgetful stage of life, is enjoying the peace and quiet of his golden years in our town—the conception of which he brought about with a single modest erection fifty years ago next month on the site of what has since been dedicated as Lord Chelmsford Park. The less said about his only human offspring and heir, Chester Grossman—undeserving owner-in-trust of our upscale Chelmsford Heights Mall—the better. And the same applies, in spades, for the ex-Mrs. Chester Grossman, whom you alluded to in your grossly ill informed article.

She, sir, for your information, is only the irresponsible owner of Fiddler's Green Cemetery—which she stole from Chester Grossman by means of divorce—and is in no other way a "contributor" to the Hall of Fame Columbarium, as you clumsily implied. To the contrary indeed, her spiteful neglect of our loved ones' remains lodged in "her" property across Trolley Street from our town is the entirely <u>negative</u> reason for our columbarium's existence! But for her ongoing malicious intent, and that of her equally unscrupulous lawyer, leftovers of many other prominent Chelmsford Heightsters would have been put up in jars at last week's dedication ceremonies — not still held hostage by her and not still the subject of unseemly haggling over ransom.

In closing, I trust you will receive these comments in the constructive spirit in which they are offered. We the people of Chelmsford Heights count on the *Weekly Weekender's* support of our upscale lifestyle, and look forward, in particular, to your publication of a Special 50th Anniversary Edition of the *Weekender*, which we of the Women's Alliance expect to be worthy of a Pulitzer Prize for its glorious historical portrayal of our distinguished town.

With sincerest best wishes,
Yours very truly,

Mrs. Phoebe Taliaferro
Chairlady-for-Life

# ONE

Crossing the Arkansas River in her yellow Checker of a car, with all her belongings in the back seat, Henryetta began to mentally compose a news article such as might appear in this week's *Weekly Weekender: Ms. Henryetta P. Hebert—correctly spelled with a 'y' because she got named after the town of Henryetta, Oklahoma, where she was born almost twenty-two years ago—has joined the Weekly Weekender staff and will be reporting on world affairs just as soon as she gets herself settled in Tulsa. In her new position as roving correspondent, Ms. Hebert will be working directly under Mr. Harold Mixon—owner, publisher and editor of the paper—just like she did back in...* No, that wasn't correct journalism, Henryetta noted to herself. For one thing, she wasn't gonna be reporting on local politics, or sports, like she did before, and she was glad of it. Her prior work on the Okmulgee County Commissioner election—not half as good as the stories put out by the *Okmulgee Tribune* and *New York Times*—must've been one of the causes of Mr. Harold havin' to close down his old newspaper, the *Henryetta Weekly Herald*, she reckoned.

And at the *Weekly Weekender* neither was she gonna be put all the way back to settin' at a desk, answering a phone and taking down classified ads that got called in, which—to be correct about it—was mainly what she did when she was the so-called editor-at-large for Mr. Harold's piddlin' little ol' newspaper dedicated to bringing "good news and good deals to the good people of Okmulgee County." When her old boss called her up last week, he told her his new big city newspaper didn't even have a Paris Flea Market section for what people in Tulsa called "crassified ads." Instead of tying her down in an office, he was gonna get her one of those Apple eye-telephones for carrying around in a pocket and taking snapshots. Mr. Harold said readers of the *Weekly Weekender* were keen as mustard about looking at pictures of what was going on in the world, so she reckoned she would be doing a lot of traveling on airplanes, 'stead of wearin' out another set of semi-new tires on her Checker.

She'd been some surprised that Mr. Harold seemed to think her newspaper training was now up to the mark, but… *In addition to her Weekly Weekender world beat, Ms. Hebert has already been assigned a major story that is going to be put in either The New York Times or USA Today. Her dream is to someday win one of those Pulitzer Prizes, so for the past two months she's been settin' in on journalism classes down at Oklahoma University in Norman, serving up food to sorority girls in the Tri Phi Phi cafeteria line, working every chance she gets on her grammar, and…*

Mr. Harold might even want to put a picture of her in the newspaper, Henryetta thought, as she made her way toward Tulsa's far southern suburbs. The most recent one she had showed her with bright red hair, big toothy smile, blue eyes with yellow sparks in 'em, and a green-and-yellow ribbon on top of her head—sorta childlike in crayon 'cause—well, his name was Duane, he was an art student, and after they'd had a tumble or two he said that Crayolas were "the only fit medium for capturing the spirit of who she was," or somethin' like that. Probably a more suitable one would be... *shown here in a flat black cap and gown at her graduation from Henryetta High School four years ago, with just slightly reddish blonde hair from her mother's side and a slightly crooked front tooth that she still has. Soon as Ms. Hebert gets some city work clothes, she'll look more...*

Seeing a sign for a "Fiddler's Green Cemetery," Henryetta steered her Checker to the side of the road. She was still miles outside the Tulsa city limits, she figured, but the next and last turn on her sheet of written directions would take her into the parking lot of a "Chelmsford Heights Mall." Some confused, she drove on in and circled—looking for a side street named Rodeo Drive—then went around the shopping center parking lot again and...Not knowing whether to scratch her watch or wind her fanny, she pulled over and waved down a good humor truck with a blinking light bulb on top and *MALL POLICE* painted on the side. A real friendly security guard, wearin' a red rubber clown nose, pointed a long red-and-white striped cane at a sign saying *Flamingo Court Entrance* and told her "Rodayoh" Drive was <u>inside</u> the mall! Beginning to feel like there might have been some kind of misunderstanding between her and Mr. Mixon—their connection wasn't so good on her old cell phone— Henryetta parked her Checker.

Off to one side of the mall entrance an old vandalized statue of a woman wearing a real straw hat, like she was a scarecrow or somethin', stood in a junkyard such as those littered along the west end of Main Street in downtown Henryetta. Might have been left over from Halloween, she thought as she walked by, but then she noticed that mixed in with a bunch of rusted old auto parts and used tires, someone was growing a vegetable garden—and a homemade sign said *Leo's Last Little Acre.* This wasn't like either one of the malls Henryetta had seen in Shawnee and Oklahoma City, not exactly. Inside, a flock of flamingo birds were hangin' by their necks over a pool of water, and in one direction she could see a bunch of stores lined up for shopping. But at her end, where she would have expected maybe a J.C. Penney's store, a big sign on a red brick wall said *YE OLDE TOWN HALL*, and below that, *Chelmsford Heights, Oklahoma.*

Henryetta peeked over a row of bushes in pots lined up on one side of the mall and saw a skinny old man, wearing a black beanie on his head and settin' in a rocking chair. "Oy!" he shouted. "Oy!" she shouted back, thinking he must be an oldtime sailor and hard of hearing or somethin'. "I'm lookin' for…"

"What, already you too got the bunions?" he asked. "So with mine you should put your own *fingers fun fus* in this tub of pickle juice."

"Maybe later," she said. "Right now I'm fixin' to be late for work, and lookin' for number 1201 on Rodayoh Drive street."

"So do the math already," the old man said, nodding the propeller stick on his beanie at a sign on the wall behind him. "This is 1205, two doors down at the *Weekly Weekender* you should be late to work."

Henryetta thanked him—then, just to be friendly, told the old codger he looked real comfortable settin' there on his front patio. He peered back at her like he thought she might be making some kind of joke. "Comfortable?" he repeated with a shrug. "Oy, I make a living."

She laughed out loud without knowing why, then saw Mr. Harold down the "street" a ways, waving to her like he'd got tumped from a boat out on Possum Pond and was sinking feet-first in mud. At that distance he looked about normal for hisself: still wearing big round eye glasses, a big bowtie, and a big…

Closer up to him, Henryetta saw that her old boss had either got hisself into a shirt that was a size too big for him or that his old neck had got even scrawnier since she'd seen him last. He hugged her like a daddy when she got to him, then led her toward a storefront that had a sign on the glass—*WEEKLY WEEKENDER*, with a motto…

"Hurry inside," Mr. Harold said, sounding kinda urgent about it.

Henryetta had never seen Mr. Harold—always so cheerful about telling "good news to good people"—look so dreadful woebegone. Right away she got a feeling she should have got rid of that old cell phone of hers after dropping it in the washing machine at the laundromat. His new newspaper's motto on the front window—spelled out stark as *Rest in Peace* on a new grave marker—promised *News of the best place and times of our lives.* Inside the *Weekender* office, on a lobby desk, she then saw a copy of last week's edition, its front page plastered with colored party pictures. And on a wall—a big map of a town called Chelmsford Heights, not Tulsa, and surrounding suburban areas, not going even as far as Tulsa, was overlaid with and odd-shaped orange cellophane blob identified as *WEEKENDER WORLD.* Her new job was gonna be no bigger and likely none better than the one she had back at the *Henryetta Weekly Herald,* she realized, as her same old skinnier boss took her into an inner office and locked the door behind them.

"Thank God you're here," Mr. Harold said, before plopping himself down behind a desk. "Henryetta, I made a terrible mistake movin' up here and buying this no account newspaper. I'm trying to get free of it, but in the meantime, I need your help real bad." No, he wasn't asking her to write up classified ads. "These stuck-uppity women around here don't mind occasional discreet notices of 'Estate Sales,'" he said, "but they've made it plain they won't tolerate garage sales that invite 'undesirable sorts' into Chelmsford Heights or...They said the Paris Flea Market section I got going for classified ads 'libelously' implied that they buy and sell used things, as opposed to fine antiques, or that they have to scrounge for cheap goods at bargain prices. They <u>hate</u> bargain prices advertised for anything, old or new!"

And no, Mr. Harold said he didn't need her to word process on a keyboard any of his ruminations that he used to write down with a pencil for his *From Where I Sit* editorials. "The people of 'Weekender World' aren't interested in reading anything in a newspaper except their own names," he said, "as headers or..." In a dither he fumbled through a pile of papers on his desk. "See for yourself," he then said, handing over what he called a "typical letter-to-the-editor," with a highlighted second paragraph: *The fault of the matter is particularly regrettable, given the sharp decline in interesting and informative pictures in the Weekender since you became editor, and your wife a "reporter." We the people of Chelmsford Heights want to know and <u>see</u> who received what civic awards at luncheons hosted by whom. We want to be told and <u>shown</u> who attended what charity events wearing what. We want to be informed of Weekend World affairs, nothing more, and always in a <u>positive</u> light supportive of our upscale lifestyle. Captions, along with photos, are generally sufficient to tell all that need be told, but only if you take much better care that we are properly identified and our names spelled correctly! As we instruct our children about their school homework, Mr. Mixon — and suggest that you emphasize to your "staff" — proof read!*

Henryetta put the letter down and Mr. Harold began to sputter: "These...these people, some of them, and their...Their proud obsession is with 'lifestyle' — as an advertising <u>adjective</u> — a descriptive term for everything that suggests a 'refined' way of life they mainly just <u>pretend</u> to be living, as…as fashion models! And they don't even know it! They're smug, shallow, pretentious, unbearably self-congratulatory and…" He carried on, getting more wound up as he went, like a Baptist preacher in a hot-as-hades revival tent, yellin' about sin or somethin' at sixty miles an hour, with gusts up to eighty. "Most of 'em are just a step or two from walking behind a mule-drawn plough, and trying too hard not to show it. The women, deep down they're ashamed to be Okies, they try to act like they're not, and some of 'em are mean as rattlesnakes. The wife's scared to leave the house to take pictures and write down names," he said, looking like he was about to break out bawling about it. "That's why I need you so bad, Henryetta — to be a roving correspondent covering Weekender World affairs, and taking pictures, while I sell fancy store ads and try to find someone who'll buy this…this sumbitch!" Henryetta was shocked, she'd never heard Mr. Harold, a regular Presbyterian church goer, say out loud such a word as sumbitch.

She was dreadful disappointed…for Mr. and Mrs. Mixon too, but… "What about that major story assignment?" she asked, hoping she might still get her journalism career halfway on track, "the one you said might get put in *The New York Times* or *USA Today*." Mr. Harold drooped down his head. "Sorry," he mumbled. The so-called major story was only a kind of history of the town of Chelmsford Heights, he said, a *Weekender* special edition to be published in July as part of a 50th anniversary celebration of the town's founding. He had intended to have her research the olden days that had never been written about — dig up some pictures and put down some brief history — and for "the modern era," go through and sorta summarize twenty-some years of *Weekly Weekenders*. "The ladies 'lifestyle' alliance has already put up half the money for the project," Mr. Harold said, looking at Henryetta with dark cloudy eyes about to sprinkle rain and maybe start to pour, "and the deadline is…I've got only three weeks! They intend to place the piece in the *Times* or *USA Today* as…as one of those infomercials like obscure 'stan' countries sometimes sponsor. The 'major story', Henryetta, it's an ad," he said, "'bout the same as you used to write up for the *Henryetta Weekly Herald*, only longer, with more pictures, lots of pictures, and names, correctly spelled names. But now even that…I'm sorry, Henryetta, honey, it's too dangerous. I can't let you do it."

Too dangerous? Henryetta like to took a pad and pencil out of her tote right then and there. But Mr. Harold nodded his head back and forth, put a finger to his lips to signal hush-hush, then got up from his chair and led her to a new-looking unpainted door at the back of his office. Henryetta followed him down a dimly lit service corridor to another door and into — she braced herself for danger — a big empty storage room. "See," Mr. Harold said, pointing at long rows of empty shelves and some cardboard scraps littered on the floor, "the *Weekly Weekender* archives — never digitized — they were here last Friday. I brought in Mrs. Taliaferro and the main ladies from the Women's Lifestyle Alliance to show 'em what we had to work with and… on Monday they were gone! Without the copies of past editions, the town's modern era history would have to be put together from scratch!" Henryetta couldn't quite see the danger in that, only the tedium. "The archives have been <u>stolen</u>," her old boss wailed, "all I have to work with are folders and folders of old photographs that were in cold storage, with some dates but no other information or <u>names</u> on the back. And the thief left a metal <u>claw</u> stuck in the wall, Henryetta, then sneaked back in the next night and retrieved the dirty weapon!"

"Have you called the police?" Henryetta asked, reaching into her canvas bag for pad and pencil. *"No!" said the agitated business owner, "the local police can't be trusted, no one in this godforsaken town can be trusted. It looks like someone doesn't want a complete 50th anniversary history of Chelmsford Heights to be dredged up, at least not by me [and the Weekly Weekender's investigative roving correspondent.]*

"I'll do it!" Henryetta said, stowing her notes. "I'll take those new party pictures to keep things goin'—and put words to the old ones too, with as many proper-spelled names as I can muster. Don't you worry none, Mr. Harold, I'll take on this sumbitch, and maybe win us a Pulitzer Prize for ad writing."

# TWO

Chester Grossman stood at a safe distance from his father's "house" in Chelmsford Heights Mall, scared to approach his old man—called Leo by one and all—who sat on his "patio" with his feet in a wash tub. They had been estranged since his father's return from the Holy Land six years ago. For the past six months they'd not even spoken to one another. And it was all his fault, Chester acknowledged, as a tear ran down his cheek. Once upon a time, he now vividly recalled, at this very spot in the mall, his dad had given him a reassuring hug and…In his troubled mind, Chester re-lived the painful memory:

*"Don't be scared, Chesty,"* his daddy said, *"Santa is just a nice old man, and he's got a very, very special present for you in that big red box up there on the back of his fire engine."*

*But he was scared, and mistrustful. Weeks ago, in his presence, his mother had shouted at his daddy that if he got "that bad boy" a Shetland pony for Christmas, she would leave their happy home and never come back. "You wouldn't want that, would you Chester?" his mother had said, after noticing he was there. "You wouldn't enjoy settin' on a dirty old furry animal 'stead of your mama's lap, would you, honey?" So now he was sure that Santa, who worked for the mall his father owned, would not give such a bad boy the Shetland pony he'd chosen over his mother's lap, 'cause she'd been gone ever since and wasn't never coming back.*

*But Leo egged him on, teasing him as usual. "Is that horse shit I smell comin' out of that crate?" he teased. "Climb on up there, boy, and see what's in that box for your enjoyment." And grudgingly, his doubts gave way. Trusting as only an innocent young boy can trust, he clambered up a ladder, across Santa's lap and onto the back of the fire engine. Tearing at the red wrapping paper, yes, he did smell horse manure, and as he pulled open the top of the big cardboard box, yes, oh yes, he felt something inside the box move, something alive that he would call Buster and put a saddle on and…To his shock and horror, his mother popped out of the box, wearing a furry coat like she'd hounded Leo to give her for Christmas. His father's loud cackle…*

Chester came out of his reverie of a traumatic Christmas past, and with a middle-aged man's now dry jaded eye, looked across the Flying Flamingos Court reflecting pool to the large block of mall space that Leo had reserved unto himself in perpetuity. The cantankerous old man resided there now, with other unappealing commercial tenants to whom he'd leased portions of his "homestead." Though his father inflicted the embarrassment upon family, mall and community out of spite, Chester, as a still wannabe dutiful son, desired a more suitable retirement home for his dad — say, an assisted living stall at the recently remodeled Greener Pastures Home out by the glue factory. As owner-in-trust and general manager of Chelmsford Heights Mall, and wannabe dutiful husband to his current wife, Shelley, he also desired to reclaim "Leo's Last Little Acre" for much needed updating of the shopping center.

Shelley, his semi-youngish third wife, was right to hound him, Chester acknowledged to himself, as he visually surveyed his surroundings. This end of the otherwise upscale mall was even worse than "so yesterday"—a term Shelley employed to describe about everything she disliked. Anyone who happened to wander in this direction would ultimately hit the bricked-up wall of a large space previously occupied by J.C. Penney's. Now, thanks to Leo's past mismanagement, the former anchor store premises—"where a Nordstrum's or Saks Fifth Avenue would be to die for," according to Shelley—served as the Chelmsford Heights town hall, with police and fire departments operating out the rear. Immediately adjacent store space, including Leo's, a chiropractor clinic and office of the *Weekly Weekender*, were deader than Kelsey's nuts—a term his father himself used to employ to describe things that were "so yesterday." And on the other side, Fanny's Fashion Boutique, an outlet for large-size women's intimate apparel—that no Chelmsford Heights woman would ever patronize except by private and confidential mail order—was the liveliest of a row of women's stores that Shelley described, quite rightly, as "so yesteryear!"

The mall, the community and she herself desperately needed something new, his wife constantly whined. They couldn't live a happy life without... "and what could be better to celebrate the Chelmsford Heights 50th anniversary than to break ground for an exciting new lifestyle shopping addition to the mall," she'd nagged for the past several months. "Chesty, don't be such an old fuddy-duddy," she'd again said this morning, before pushing him away. "Today's Chelmsford Heights woman wants things that say to the world—This is me, this is my upscale lifestyle!" And then, as he was leaving their recently redecorated *boudoir-avec-Marie Antoinette bidet*... "For heaven's sake, Chester," she'd said, "all you ever think about is sex and money!" And Shelley was right about that too, Chester had to admit. Unless he could get control of

Leo's Last Little Acre, he would likely worry himself to death about going broke and becoming even more "so yesterday" in her Louis XIV bed.

His father's preserve was the only conceivable site for an addition to the mall. And the old man as his former self, in his right mind and not consumed with paternal disappointment, would have been all for building more income-producing space. In his prime, he'd been solely consumed with making money, and in later years had became absolutely paranoid about not letting the IRS take any of it from him. Dad-blame-it! The misunderstanding that ruined their relationship was partly his father's fault, and his mother's, Chester silently whined. A few years before her death, they deceitfully got divorced—amicably, as part of a cockeyed tax avoidance scheme that only incidentally made their only child, Chester, his mother's sole heir. And after her passing, Leo, again for tax reasons, had put in trust for Chester's keeping his entire worldly estate—mainly comprised of the mall he'd built as a younger man and the Fiddler's Green Cemetery across Trolley Street. Still worried about paying taxes, he'd then immigrated to Israel, claiming a right to citizenship based on his being part Cherokee and thus a member of "a lost Hebrew tribe." After two years over there, his "right of return" denied, Leo had come back to find…

Chester instinctively ducked behind one of the mall's faux Greek columns to avoid risk of being seen by his father, who had gotten up from his foot soak and was now hanging socks on a wire strung between two potted Ficus trees. The old coot had come back from Israel, crazy as a cuckoo—and mad as a cuckold to find that not only could Chester not return legal ownership of the mall to him without life threatening tax consequences to them both, and had lost ownership of the cemetery in a divorce settlement with his second wife, Evylene, but also...Dad-gum-it! He had acted as his own lawyer in the divorce, and as the old saying sort of went, the other one of them had turned out to be an incompetent fool.

Somewhat in the mold of Oklahoma's own Will Rogers from up the road in Claremore—famous for saying he'd never met a man he didn't like—Chester had never met a man, or woman, he didn't desperately want to like him. Dreading the unpleasantness of confrontation and litigation, he'd bent over backwards to calm down Evylene—frontwards and facing backwards, it now seemed, to satisfy her lawyer—and in the nerve wracking process of all that bending he'd made a small clerical error, in effect. By signing a document conveying all his right, title and interest in the Fiddler's Green Cemetery property, he'd inadvertently given to his ex-wife not only the cemetery real estate *per se*, but also the buried remains of his mother, Pearl Grossman, that he'd unknowingly acquired by inheritance as her sole heir. Afterward, realizing his mistake when he'd sought to disinter his mom, he'd been shocked that the once so sweet Evylene could still be so vindictive about...about his relationship with Shelley, and so uncaring about the second-hand effect of her smoking rage on Leo. More than anything else, it was Evylene's grudge and greed and grotesque sense of humor that had resulted in the ongoing father-and-son estrangement standing in the way of Shelley's dream of getting a so-called "lifestyle" addition to the mall—not to mention his own dream of getting laid. Unless he could make peace...

Noticing that his father had left his post, Chester screwed up his courage, then hurried out a side entrance toward the old man's "garden" on the backside of his residential store space. Once outside, however, seeing Leo, leaning on a shovel and looking—wistfully, it seemed—at a memorial…Chester's sentimental nature again took him back, this time to their last face-to-face encounter six months ago, when he'd stood in this very same spot and…*He was giddy as an innocent young boy on Christmas Eve, not about getting a Shetland pony or anything else for himself, but about giving something back to his aged father—and winning his forgiveness. Leo would be so surprised, so delighted to… He himself was surprised, stunned in fact, to behold his fifty-thousand dollar birthday present to his dear old dad: a large box, lying on the back of a flatbed truck equipped with a wench, beautifully wrapped in floral-patterned paper and tied with an enormous pink ribbon.*

*"Oy!" the startled birthday boy shouted, as the wench operator hoisted the big gift box into the air above his patch of weeds. "Damnit, I said OY!" his father again shouted, obviously trying to make himself heard over the tooting of the brass band hired for the occasion. People began to gather. The mood became festive. A photographer from the Weekly Weekender clicked her camera to capture the happy moment. He approached his father, waved for the band to stop blasting "Happy Birthday to You," and tried, unsuccessfully, to give the confused old man a hug. "Father," he said, arms still wide open—as the box containing his mother's remains landed on the ground with a hard thud—"It's Mom! I got her back—as a memorial memento for your enjoyment. Now, you old codger, you, give your son a big ol'…" Wild eyed with excitement, his father, eighty- years-old to the day, tore at the floral wrapping like a kid getting a coveted, albeit deceased, Shetland pony. With shovel in hand, he began pry loose the lid of the wooden packing crate, then went to work inside the box, no doubt carried away with…*

*"No! No! No!" he yelled to his father. "Leo, stop it! She's…She's bound to have…changed. The years underground have taken their toll and…" Stuffing flew out of the box, surely to reveal only a sealed coffin,*

*but…His father lurched backward, horror on his wizened face, then looked up to heaven above, his arms raised to God… "DUMKOPT!" he wailed. "For a son You send me a dumkopt! And a mossik! Oy, oy is me."*

*Though also horrified, as well as feeling unappreciated, he went to his father's side. In the open box…He too looked up to God with uplifted arms. "It's not my fault!" he cried out. "It's…It's that damned wench that's to blame!"*

Chester again returned from his memories of the regrettable past, shaken by the sight he'd recalled—in the box, her rock-hard body covered with bird droppings, her arms broken off, had lain a statue of the Venus de Milo, her pedestal inscribed *Pearl Conan Grossman*. Evylene, that heartless wench, had tricked him again, this time by taking his money and delivering to his father as a memorial memento—not his mother's bodily remains, as ordered and paid for—but the headstone that had marked her grave in Fiddler's Green Cemetery. And a middle-aged woman from the *Weekly Weekender* had been there to record and preserve forever yet another of his public humiliations, Chester recalled, turning away from Leo's junkyard, where the memento would taunt him every time he passed this way.

The circumstances were still not right for seeking a reconciliation with his father, Chester decided. He had nothing to offer. First, he had to get back at—without mercy or regard for law and order this time—the "<u>Evil</u>ene One." All Chester wanted—for Shelley—was a happy married life, even if he had to spend his part in it locked up in prison.

# THREE

At the sight of one of her off-duty subordinates waving to her as he exited a screened Chelmsford Heights Mall truck dock, Chief Rosemary O'Connor backed her police motorcycle deeper into a clump of bushes on the perimeter of the shopping center parking lot. She was on a stake out. To be seen by anyone other than a fellow officer would jeopardize her covert operation. And quite possibly result in a regrettable loss of life. The chief, told she resembled Rosie O'Donnell and therefor commonly known as "Bulldog" since her army days, had a nose for odious plots afoot in Chelmsford Heights, as well as those hatched in bad novels. Once she caught the scent of something not quite kosher, she followed the odor to its rotten core, no matter how many pages she had to turn.

An hour and a half ago she'd spotted a yellow Checker cab circling the mall, its driver obviously casing the joint for a heist or, just as strongly discouraged in Chelmsford Heights, cruising for a fare. She'd as good as had the goods on the wise guy but, dad-gum-it, she wasn't allowed to set foot or wheel on Chester Grossman's property, except to go back and forth to and from police headquarters. Chester was a sissy in Bulldog's book, yellow as mustard without the bite, and currently wetting his pants about getting drawn into a pending lawsuit against her and the town, even though...Hells bells, she'd had good reason to suspect shoplifting was afoot, and had crossed Trolley Street into the neighboring town of Fiddler's Green in hot pursuit of a prime suspect. In line with sound police procedure, she'd riddled the tires of the getaway car with multiple bursts from her automatic weapon—to make good and sure it stayed good and stopped in the driveway of a house on Apple Street. She'd made the collar by the book—forcing the perp from the disabled vehicle at gunpoint, then to the ground, before cuffing her arms behind her back and a leg to a nearby post. None of the little children in the car were hurt, just a little scared and no doubt disappointed that their grandma was likely headed for the slammer.

She'd got no medal, and no publicity for her heroic deed. In fact, the mayoress, Mrs. Taliaferro, super-sensitive about press coverage of community affairs—reportedly because of a sensational *Weekly Weekender* story about a semi-scandal years ago—suppressed any account of the incident. But most of the citizens of Chelmsford Heights—who didn't like Fiddlers coming to their mall even to just plain ol' shop—they heard all about what happened and had her backside covered when questions came up about the missing evidence stolen from Fanny's Fashion Boutique. Not Chester, though; he backed down. And now the innocent citizens of Chelmsford Heights were paying the price for him bringing in a bunch of clowns to handle mall security. Bulldog had seen one of the jokers at least make a stop of the suspicious yellow Checker but, armed with only a plastic cane, he'd backed off without even searching the cab for... "Yo, Bulldog!" someone yelled from a passing truck, "bow-wow-wow!" She appreciated the friendly shout-out, but decided she'd better move to a more hidden post, and while she was at it, take a whiz.

Inside the Chew-n-Choke at Fiddler's Green—called a truck stop cafe to suggest ambience—Bulldog waved to a waitress behind the counter, as she headed for the can. She had nothing personal against the folks on the "dirty side" of Trolley Street. Residents of Fiddler's Green and those who worked there were more her kind of people than the snoots of Chelmsford Heights. But she was a professional, dedicated to upholding law and order wherever she found it, and the Fiddler's Green police department didn't even have a motorcycle. As Chelmsford Heights Chief, on the other hand, she had fifteen well equipped, well uniformed and well armed men under her command, plus dispatchers and other office staff.

The town could well afford such a security force, and then some. It was less than three square miles in size with a population of only about 4,000 residents, but the mall paid jillions of dollars in sales taxes and there was nothing the well-fixed Heightsters wanted that they couldn't afford to buy—including large ornamental iron gates at the main yellow-bricked road into town, antique street lamps from Europe, lavishly landscaped parks with statues and fountains, trucked-in spring water from the Ozark Mountains for everyday flushing, all kinds of decorations for major and minor holidays, festivals, parades and other such events. And this summer, gates were to be installed at all town entrances 'cause—more or less in the words of the mayoress, Mrs. Taliaferro—the good people of Chelmsford Heights not only wanted to feel safe and secure, but also wanted to feel separated and apart from unfortunate others who did not appreciate an upscale way of life. The town didn't have schools and churches requiring any public subsidies, only a country club and golf course.

Fiddler's Green, on the other hand, about the same size town…Though anxious to get back to her surveillance of the suspicious yellow Checker, on her way out of the Chew-n-Choke, Chief O'Connor felt obliged to pay her respects to a professional colleague seated at the lunch counter. "Pop" Barnett was Chief and sole member of the Fiddler's force, having retired several years ago from duty as a school-crossing attendant in Tulsa. He regularly worked only the graveyard shift, patrolling the south lane of Trolley Street—along what was sometimes called the "Mason-Dixon Line"—keeping an eye ball on traffic, and jaw jacking with truckers on the CB like it was still the 1970's.

"How's your hammer hangin', Pop?" she asked, setting her Big Behind on a naugahyde-covered stool next to his. "Bent for Lent," the old man replied, same as always. "How's your paper-hangin', Bulldog?" he asked, referring to the number of "blue slips" she'd issued to speeders in the north, Chelmsford Heights lane of Trolley Street. "Only fair to middling'," she answered with a sigh. "Life, it do get daily in the slow lane."

"Yeah, I ain't read much about you lately in that *Police Blotter* section of that *Weekender* paper," Pop said. "Course we only get 'em here after they been tore up and stained with spilled forty-weight. You oughta work the darktime, like me," her fellow law enforcement officer said. "With this heat we're havin', lots o' strange things goin' on around here, on <u>both</u> sides of the tracks."

"Oh yeah?" said Bulldog, catching the scent of something possibly foul. Ordinarily, despite having only one cop and only one police vehicle, Fiddler's Green was utterly free of crime. "Have a cup o' forty-weight and a mud ball," Pop said, "I'll put you wise to some of my suspicions about what the Masons are up to." Though tempted to linger for coffee and a donut, Chief Bulldog got up from the stool and rubbed her big belly. "Wish I could, but...gotta cut the coax, Pop. I'll catch you on the backside."

"Some yahoos slashed the tires on my black-and-white while I was on duty," her good buddy nevertheless continued, as Bulldog snapped the chin-strap of her motorcycle helmet. "I'll be on stationary patrol in front of the locked-up pearly gates at the corner of the cemetery 'til further notice. I'm pretty sure it was Masons from the Heights, snatching bodies to put up in their jars, accordin' to our newspaper, *The Guillotine*. Or it might've been my late ex-wife, Irene, who..."

Bulldog had to tune him out, dang it.

Back on her police hog and back across Trolley Street, she silently cursed her dang luck. She would have liked to jaw jack with Pop about what was going on at darktime on <u>both</u> sides of the tracks, but at the moment she had other likely crime in progress to...The chief spotted the yellow Checker coming out of the mall parking lot, trying to make a run for it but headed right at her. She swerved into the oncoming lane, dropped her motorcycle onto the yellow bricks, and drew her gun from its holster. The getaway cab screeched to a halt in front of her. Without lowering her weapon or taking her eyes off the would-be fugitive in the driver's seat, she cautiously circled to the side of the Checker. "Welcome to Chelmsford Heights"—that was Bulldog's trademark line for making a collar—delivered this time to a little strawberry-blonde caucasian female with a slightly crooked front tooth, who had already rolled down the car window. "Now, get out of the vehicle nice and slow, with your hands up in the air where I can see 'em."

31

What in tarnation?!" said the suspect, jumping out of the cab like her hair was on fire, with her face breaking out in freckles. "I like to ran right into you, you dang fool!"

Bulldog retreated several steps and clicked on the police radio attached to a shoulder strap. "Back-up! Back-up! ASAP!" she shouted. "Ten-Twenty: intersection of Benson and Hedges. Arresting officer needs back-up, on the double!"

"Why is it you're the one so dandered up?" the deranged taxi driver demanded, shaking a fist. "I'm the one drivin' around without no insurance!"

The situation was spinning out of control, but Bulldog... "Oh my god!" she cried out. The bare foot of a body in the back seat of the cab had been jolted forward over the front seat headrest, and in the air...Bulldog caught a sickening whiff of...vinegar? "Oy," said a voice, startling the suspect too, it seemed. "For comfort, a bus I shoulda took."

But no harm, no foul, Chief O'Connor was relieved to say to herself thirty minutes later. Innocent mistakes were made by all concerned parties and, unregrettably, the result was not fatal but favorable. With Mr. Leo Grossman behind her on her police cycle, she'd blown past Chester Grossman's rinky-dink security guard with nary a by-your-leave. Mr. Leo's "Last Little Acre" was his legal residence, she was duty-bound to cross the mall parking lot to take the confused old man home. Though it was widely known that Chester and his father were still at odds with one another due to some kind of misunderstanding arising from one of Chester's divorces, she couldn't help but believe that the prodigal son would be grateful that she'd thwarted what might have developed into a ransom demand by...someone... maybe his ex-wife, who Chester had publicly accused — only about six months ago — of being a body snatcher.

And now, as a bonus of sorts, with Mr. Leo back to puttering in his vegetable garden, the coast was clear for a quick inspection of a suspicious smelling dumpster area in a nearby truck dock. Bulldog knew the likely crime scene well from past fruitless investigations. Though smoking, along with chewing and dipping, was technically not a major felony in Chelmsford Heights, the mayoress had issued a proclamation saying the vice was "strongly discouraged," and some hardened criminals...Aha! Having expected as much, Chief O'Connor knelt over the foul evidence and, with rubber-gloved hands, carefully collected ten butts, all of them Marlboros! Dog-gone-it, now that she thought about it, that little What's-Her-Name who said she worked for the *Weekender* had parked her yellow cab near here and... Bulldog detected — no doubt about it — snatching of bodies, dead or alive, had spread from Fiddler's Green and was now afoot in Chelmsford Heights.

# FOUR

In his storefront office next door to the Chew-n-Choke truck stop cafe, Willis "Versus" Willis sat at his desk, gazing into space and making a "steeple" with the fingers of both his hands. Forty years ago, he had set out to be just a plain ol' country lawyer, helping folks with their problems, and he'd found it useful and rewarding to continue playing the part. Of a morning he would put on a baggy suit, discreetly stained here and there, then look into a mirror and practice a down-home way of talking: "Yessir, I'm just a country lawyer, doin' what I can to he'p as many folks as I can git their own day in court, or even two or three days, if that's what it takes to set thangs right," he might say, before going to work, all fired up to sue some sumbitch. But today… Willis couldn't decide what to do about Chester Grossman.

He had nothing personal against Chester, no more than against the hundreds of other poor saps he'd sued through the years, or the dozens of life's losers he'd filed multiple lawsuits against. On the other hand, he had to make a living like everybody else, and like most businesses, country lawyerin', he'd found, required a fella to take advantage of other people's mistakes and misfortunes whenever such fortuitous opportunities presented themselves. And Chester Grossman, he'd found, was a walking-and-talking "opportunity" personified. Not that he'd ever "targeted" the sitting duck with a bull's eye on his chest. No, Willis mainly handled divorces for pissed off wives who thought the legal process had to do with righting wrongs, 'stead of just dividing up the pots-and-pans left over from the feast of love-and-lust. Only by happenstance—maybe nudged some by his TV ads and billboards—Evylene Grossman had walked into his office seven years ago, and such was <u>her</u> greed and thirst for vengeance, she'd effectively still not left. Hardly a month had passed since then that she hadn't called from some distant place, asking him to deal with yet other contentious issues related to her divorce settlement with Chester. Willis grappled more or less constantly with the ex-husband, his father, Leo, and with numerous of their friends and neighbors in Chelmsford Heights about matters involving Evylene's ownership of Fiddler's Green Cemetery.

To maintain her high-flying lifestyle, his client had milked the property. Due to her imprudent management, questionable accounting practices, some bad luck and maybe some bad advice now and then, the cemetery's legally required maintenance fund had long been woefully inadequate for its purpose. New sales of burial plots were non-existent, net value of the asset was a small fraction of what it used to be. The people of Chelmsford Heights, as the old joke sorta went—Chester and Leo Grossman, in particular—were dying to get <u>out</u>, or rather dying to retrieve the remains of departed loved ones from the weedy burial ground on the "dirty side" of Trolley Street. Recently, the Chelmsford Heights Women's Alliance for Upscale Lifestyle, Liberty and Pursuit of Happiness had completed construction of a columbarium wing of the town's Hall of Fame, for deposit of the ashes of their recovered and cremated late grandparents, parents, uncles and aunts, husbands and wives. But because of unstable soil conditions, missing or vandalized headstones, poor record keeping, regulatory red tape and various legal considerations, removal of graves from Fiddler's Green was not all that simple a process—and Evylene had made sort of a business out of the difficulties.

Except for her own profit, she wasn't much inclined to be accommodating toward the ladies of Chelmsford Heights, who had snubbed her during her marriage to Chester. "I doubt the old bats have changed much," she'd said through the phone about a year ago, "but even by having a look at their corpses first, how can we be sure who's who, and who belongs to whom?" And of course she took special delight in biting the hand of her ex-husband, Chester who'd practically handed the cemetery property to her in a gift-wrapped box—out of fear she would burn down Chelmsford Heights Mall, he said—and by acting as his own lawyer in their divorce. The dang fool…

"What's it gonna be, Willis?" asked his youngish, dark-haired paralegal assistant, Clara, from the open doorway to his office. "Do we need another file cabinet for Grossman cases, or are you gonna give the dumb bastard a pass this time?"

Willis ignored her and continued to steeple. Though he'd gotten the name "Versus" for the countless times his formal name had appeared as plaintiff's attorney at the top of court petitions versus others, he was conflicted about whether to name Chester Grossman and the Chelmsford Heights Mall as co-defendants in a new lawsuit against the Town of Chelmsford Heights and its Chief of Police. Chester's shared legal responsibility for the wrongful, brutal arrest of an old woman—now Willis' client— would not be easy to establish, and might not be worth the trouble.

Like Evylene and her careless handling of the Fiddler's Green Cemetery, Chester had drained the mall's coffers to support the upscale lifestyle of the current Mrs. Grossman. Mortgage debt on the aging commercial property, like that on their recently re-done Chelmsford Heights "chateau" and weekend house on Grand Lake, was pert near up to the eaves, Willis knew. And if driven into bankruptcy and likely another divorce, who could say what a desperate man such as Chester Grossman might do in retaliation against his perceived tormentor?

Evylene's most recent dirty trick, and his too, Willis would have to admit…To have again, for a second time, taken advantage of the lawyerless fool's genteel affectation, his dainty mincing of words, and his ambiguous offer of fifty thousand dollars for "the memorial memento"of his mother in Evylene's possession — well, he deserved what he got his father for a birthday present: a statue of a woman that had marked his mother's grave instead of her remains. And that may have pushed Chester to or beyond his limit, Willis feared. In response, the aggrieved ex-husband and no doubt disappointed gift-giver had already filed a lawsuit against him, <u>personally</u>, and had lodged a complaint with the Oklahoma Bar Association for "fraud, multiple acts of professional malfeasance, and grave robbery by my ex-wife's crooked country lawyer, Willis 'Versus' Willis, Esquire." Having been burned twice, to now again be confronted by… "Let me think about it," he said to Clara, still standing in the doorway, now smoking a cigarette and eyeing him with unconcealed contempt.

Willis searched a pile of papers on his desk. In connection with the lawsuit he'd filed against Chelmsford Heights and Chief O'Connor, he'd taken Chester's deposition. And the danged fool, dumb as a fence post, had again shown up as his own lawyer, with little knowledge of...Willis found the transcript of their question-and-answer encounter and began to read:

**Q.** Ain't it true, Mr. Grossman...

**A.** Call me Chester. Let's be friendly and leave our other differences out of this, please.

**Q.** Ain't it true, Chester, that prior to this here incident we're talkin' about, the Chelmsford Heights Mall employed no security personnel of its own?

**A.** Well, Willis, I myself patrol the mall on a daily basis, and no additional law enforcement is needed. I have very specific rules for what conduct is and is not allowed on the premises.

**Q.** But Chester, you also count on officers of the Chelmsford Heights police to enforce your rules, ain't that so?

**A.** I repeat, no enforcement, as you call it, is needed. The mall is upscale, the rules are clear that...No eating outside the food court, for instance, that's very, very, very strongly discouraged. If you read our local newspaper's *Police Blotter*, you won't find news of any criminal activity whatsoever in...

**Q.** But ain't it right, Chester, that it was you your own self who saw a Ms. Fanny O'Brien come runnin' out of her underwear boutique, yellin' "Robbery!" and you your own self who shouted, "Call Security!"?

**A.** I don't recall. There was a great deal of panic. I had to cope with panic. Is the air conditioning on in here?

**Q.** But Chester, ol' friend...

**A.** Mr. Grossman to you, plus Esquire! I'm my own attorney, just like you.

**Q.** Okay, Mr. Grossman, Esquire, didn't you your own self walkie-talkie to, and personally instruct the Chelmsford Heights Chief of Police to, quote, "Put out an All Points Bulletin for capture of a woman you saw fleeing, believed to be armed and dangerous"?

**A.** As I said, Mr. Willis Willis, Esquire, it was not a time when one knows what one says. God, it's hot in here.

**Q.** Ain't it the truth, Mr. Grossman, Esquire, that Chief of Police O'Connor was actin' on your personal instruction when she chased down my client, off mall premises and beyond town limits to arrest the poor woman for...

**A.** The woman may have been smoking, or dipping, both are strongly discouraged throughout Chelmsford Heights. Whatever the police did, or didn't do, they were acting in response to a private citizen's cry for help, not to <u>me</u> as owner only in-trust and as only <u>general</u> manager of the mall. Lots of people cry for help, not just me, all the time.

**Q.** Alright, but you do admit, don't you, that right after this happened you <u>did</u> hire and deploy a squad of...

**A.** I admit no such thing. They're unarmed clowns, brought in for the summer to hand out balloons to childish shoppers.

**Q.** But their vehicles and, uh, "costumes" are imprinted, in large letters—MALL POLICE—ain't they?

**A.** Well, if they are, it's...it's a typo. What are you going to do about it, Mr. Shyster, sue me? Strike that, forget I said... "sue me," please.

**Q.** So Mr. Grossman, Esquire, if you again, God forbid, saw a grandmother you thought might be shoplifting, you would not "cry out" to one of your clowns to make an arrest?

**A.** Certainly not. The mall itself and I personally have no…no specific rule against that particular activity. I don't know about the town…And may I remind you, as a lawyer should know, many courts have ruled that malls are <u>public</u> places, for citizen assembly, free speech and…and so for police brutality. My mall is named after a very famous public street in Beverly Hills, California. So it was perfectly fitting and understandable for Chelmsford Heights police to patrol it, if they did, by mistake! So there!

**MR. WILLIS:** Let the record show that the witness is shaking his fist at me and mouthing silent threats.

**MR. GROSSMAN:** I was stretching my jaw, I recently got an electro-lifestyle lift and… I was only signaling for another pitcher of water. Let the record show that this man, Mr. Willis Willis, <u>Un</u>esquire should be disbarred for robbing innocent graves!

**Q.** Speakin' of robbery, Mr. Grossman, Esquire, when Ms. Fanny O'Brien yelled that word <u>at</u> you, she was complainin'— not about any shopliftin' goin' on, but about a bill for air conditioning that she got from you, her landlord, ain't that right?

**A.** A clerical error, as it turned out, nothing more sinister than a billing…<u>I'm</u> not the typo cheat here and would never…Would someone <u>please</u> open a window in this hell hole!?

**Q.** But it was you, and just you, in panic, who jumped to the conclusion my client was shopliftin', aint that so?

**A.** It so happens that I am a proud active member of the Chelmsford Heights Neighborhood Watch. I simply reported suspicious behavior to the police because I was not personally armed.

**Q.** What suspicious behavior?
**A.** What?

**Q.** What did you see, hear or smell that made you suspect women's underwear was bein' shoplifted in your mall that has no rule against it?

**MR. WILLIS:** Let the record show that the witness is now standin', holdin' his chair above his head and threatenin' to...
**MR. GROSSMAN:** Let the record show that I am simply moving my chair closer to the air conditioning, and that this madman himself is standing...
**MR. WILLIS:** Let the record show that Mr. Grossman, Esquire, is runnin' toward the door without bein' excused.

Willis put down the transcript, still not decided about what to do. Chester Grossman was spineless, he reckoned, as well as dumb as...But that didn't necessarily mean he wasn't dangerous as barbed wire strung too taut to a worm-eaten post. And the sumbitch might become even more stressed if...Before he went to trial, Willis planned to soften up the Town of Chelmsford Heights with at least the threat of an artillery barrage of sorts. Civic leaders over there were keenly vulnerable to even pot shots of bad publicity that besmirched their refined upscale image of themselves, and in his files from many other cases Willis had lots of ammunition. More "bodies" were buried across Trolley Street than in Fiddler's Green Cemetery, and he knew who, where and approximately why a bunch of 'em were resting, so far, in peace. But the trial or settlement of the wrongful arrest case was still a ways in the future and...Willis called out to Clara, who instantly reappeared in the doorway. "Let's not start another Grossman case," he said, "at least not yet. Let's let the dumb bastard twist in the wind awhile longer, and see which way he blows."

# FIVE

Henryetta woke up in the cozy bedroom of a fully furnished rent house that Mr. Harold had got for her. It was located in a neighborhood—a little town itself actually, called Fiddler's Green—right across a busy street from Chelmsford Heights Mall, but not included in the orange blob on the map in the *Weekly Weekender* office. And now Henryetta, looking out a picture window, sort of understood why it got left out. All the houses along the narrow street she was on were lots smaller than the ones she'd seen yesterday on a tour of Chelmsford Heights and other parts of so-called "Weekender World." Like the little bungalow she was standing in, all the attached garages over here looked like they'd been remodeled into knotty pine dens or maybe bedrooms for young'ns. The street out front—Peach Street—looked like the Walmart parking lot back in Henryetta. A least half the trucks were company-owned, and lots of the cars had signs painted on 'em too. Fiddler's Green was home to working people, well-to-do folks lived in Chelmsford Heights and other suburbs. Not that the difference in worldly comforts much mattered at the end of things, Henryetta noted, as she saw a black hearse come down the street, stop, then slowly back into the driveway of what looked like, now, an empty little house across the way.

Later, inside the mall, she reckoned that the darkened residence of Mr. Leo Grossman at 1205 Rodeo Drive might be "empty" too. She'd banged on the glass storefront door, but… Henryetta spit into the palm of her left hand to perish the thought. She sure hoped, for her own sake, that the old man was still just asleep and hadn't up and passed away after gettin' hauled off on a police motorcycle yesterday. According to Mr. Harold, his mall neighbor was likely to be her best source for history of the pre *Weekly Weekender* early days of Chelmsford Heights that the Women's Lifestyle Alliance wanted so bad to get put in *The New York Times* or *USA Today*. Mr. Leo was the conceiver and founder of the town, according to Mr. Harold, and founding father of the Town of Fiddler's Green too, but she wasn't supposed to waste her time on the "other side" of the street. "The old man's a character," Mr. Harold had said. "He tries to speak Yiddish, but butchers it somethin' awful. His son, Chester, says the family is part Cherokee, not Hebrew and…He's reached that forgetful age, Henryetta, and is likely to varnish the facts, I expect, so you'll have to listen carefully to his recollections to get at the true history of this proud 'upscale' place."

Henryetta banged on the door again. She'd reckoned from the git go that the lanky old man wearing a beanie — him settin' there with his feet in a tub of vinegar — might have got to be a little on the forgetful side. She'd never known of anyone doin' that for a bunion, or set up housekeeping in a shopping mall neither. And him hiding in the back seat of her Checker under her bedding, fixin' to do Lord knew what with a shovel…Reminded of the sign for "Leo's Last Little Acre," Henryetta walked out of the mall the way she came in yesterday. And sure enough, beside the broke-up statue of a woman wearing about nothin' but a straw hat—its pedestal inscribed *Pearl Conan Grossman*—she found Mr. Leo in his junkyard garden, propped up on one of those sunbathing cots in nothin' hisself 'cept undershorts—reading out loud from a book. "Oy!" she said, and just to be friendly: "How's the used tire bidness?"

The old man looked up over his reader glasses, then thumbed through his book. "So how should I know from chopped liver about the used tire business?" he then said. "I'm a *moyl*, my trade is strictly circumcisions."

*Moyl?* Circumcisions? "But…what you got on display here is used tires," said Henryetta. "So I just thought…"

"So, if you was a *moyl*, what would you display?" he said, with a kind of skeleton-like big-toothed grin. She laughed, without knowing exactly why, and the…the *moyl* invited her to set down in a lawn chair. His book, she noticed, was titled *Joys of Yiddish* by a writer named Leo… "Rosten," said the present Mr. Leo, putting the book aside, "he teaches the language of our fodders by writing down jokes." Feeling like Mr. Leo's Yiddish might not be so butchered, and the foreign language not so hard to understand after all, Henryetta explained her assignment, took pad and pencil out of a pocket, a folder of old *Weekender* photos from a tote, but…

"History, schmistory," Mr. Leo said. "People re-make-up the past to suit their own opinions…of themselves mainly—and *bubbe,* for you to try to tell 'em something they don't want to hear already, it might be dangerous." But Henryetta persisted, promising she would only ask about facts and would not write down any opinions. "First thing," she said, "as founding fodder, why was it you named this here town Chelmsford Heights?

'Cause, for the life of me, I don't see no high ground around here and..."

"I didn't," he said. "Hanzeltown, I named the town already, and across Trolley Street I called the other one Greteltown — for Hanzel and Gretel, my two meanest guard dogs. The Chelmsfolk themselves, later they re-named the town and all the streets to suit their sense of an 'upscale' way of life."

Henryetta searched her folder and came up with a photo, marked "Town Namesake" on the back. On the front it showed a big statue of a man up on a rearin' horse, waving a hat in the air. He looked like George Washington to her, but a pedestal inscription said he was *LORD CHELMSFORD 1827 - 1905.* And according to the inscription it must have been the Lord, or else — also etched — *Peter O'Toole in Zulu Dawn, 1979* — who must have spoke the words that seemed to have been adopted as the town's motto: *Learn nothing from that Irishman except how not to behave.*

Mr. Leo like to died laughing, then handed the picture back to her. "My son, Chester, he's Irish. But no, *bubbe*," he said, dabbing his teared up eyes with the backs of his bony hands, "the Chelmfolk, they named their town after the <u>mall</u> already, then put up the statue of that Englishman they afterward looked up in a book. Moe Goldberg, such a businessman — he owned Goldberg's, the local Tulsa department store where we now got Macy's — he'd picked 'Chelmsford' for the mall — off the label of an apricot jam jar, he said, 'cause he knew that to Hanzeltown alrightniks it would sound like an outlet for better-priced goods from 'up market' England. 'Buy Yiddish, sell British,' that was Moe Goldberg's motto. Such a *mossik*, oy, such a prank he played on the town *goyim*. See, *bubbe*," Mr. Leo continued, with another skeletal grin, "'Chelm', I found out later, is a name in Jewish mythology for a town populated entirely by fools."

"Is that 'goyem' with an 'e', or 'goyim' with an 'i'?" Henryetta asked. "'Cause, you know, to a red dirt girl like me they sound just alike."

"For this bunch, I'd use a big 'I'," he said, with a chuckle, "<u>underlined</u>. And as for the streets of the town, the Chelmfolk, they named them for the brands of the cigarettes they smoked to look, uh, 'British'," the forgetful old man said, and Henryetta jotted, "and stuck on other English terms for…well, now already we got Winston <u>Way</u>. Dunhill <u>Drive</u>, Chesterfield <u>Court</u>—all 'up market' to that Okie way of hearin' you mentioned."

"What was it you first named the streets of Greteltown, somethin' like 'Gingerbread Lane'?" Henryetta asked, having some fun and maybe trying to be a little bit clever. And Mr. Leo did chuckle some. "No, *tchotse*," he said, "I named the streets after trees, 'cause we had not so many of 'em out here on the prairie, and…"He rubbed the silver stubble on his chin. "Now that I think about it, I 'spect that's why these other red-dirt-niks around here, just like me, stuck 'Heights' onto the town name."

Starting to sound to Henryetta not so Yiddish, more just plain Okie, Mr. Leo went on to say that he wasn't really the founder of Chelmsford Heights and Fiddler's Green. It was his daddy who bought up most of the land where both towns now set—for farming, but with instructions in his will that it be chopped up into residential lots after he was gone. "'Buy wholesale, sell retail,'" Pappy said—"except for the two best corners that he wanted kept for the family businesses: an auto salvage yard over here and and a garbage dump on the other corner. I promised I'd keep 'em goin', but…" Mr. Leo got a kinda faraway look in his black eyes, Henryetta noted. "Goldberg's came along, wantin' a piece on this side for a branch department store," he then said, "and people were willin' to pay five hundred dollars a load to dump remains of loved ones over yonder, so…Do the math already: with some of 'em stacked, that was almost a million bucks an acre back then."

"So I reckon the folks over in Greteltown re-named their town after Fiddler's Green Cemetery," Henryetta ventured, afield from her assignment but interested anyway. "But I'd still say you were the fodder of these towns, Mr. Leo, you're just gettin' a little for… a little modest in your old…in your old undershorts you got on today."

"No, already it was for a Tavern on Trolley Street they were calling the town Fiddler's Green," he said. "But I <u>was</u> the founding fodder of food courts, *bubbe,* you can put that fact down in history. Notice no onions you were smelling in the mall?" He explained that fast food "joints" used to be scattered all through malls "like shoe stores," and that his wife — "Pearl, *aleha ha-sholem,* always she was *kvetching* about the food odors putting her out of the mood for clothes shopping." Henryetta, liking the notion that a Mrs. Leo had been his inspiration for the idea of food courts, scribbled the fact into her notebook, along with a caption for a photograph — *Chelmsford Heights First Couple* — if she could get the old man to stand up for a picture of him beside the wife's statue — and if not… "So Mrs Grossman was 'Mudder of Food Courts,'" she said, trying out an alternative caption for just a statue picture. He looked at her, maybe like he thought she was making a joke. "Oy," he said, "I was in the embrace of another woman, a…a *baleboste* at the time. A bossy bitch who made me do it, she was my 'inspiration'." Henryetta, though shocked and disappointed, asked for the name of the historically important bossy bitch. "'Miss Necessity'," the old man said. "<u>She</u> was the mudder of my food court invention."

Mr. Leo said that after he made a "loss-leader lease" of land to J.C. Penney at the other end of the "dumbbell" from Goldberg's—"that's what they called malls back then," he explained, "dumbbells, weighted at both ends by department stores"—he discovered he didn't have enough land left to build enough money-making small-store space in the middle. "Oy! such a *bulbenik* to foul things up like that," he said, smacking a palm against his forehead. "And all the experts, including Moe Goldberg, they told me: 'Leo,' they said, 'are you *meshuge*? You should drop dead before even thinking of putting a block of space for shopping on a second-level add-on to the dumbbell not connected to department stores, you *dumkopt*. Women, they won't go off-level, up or down even for sale-priced goods!' And the experts were right, I knew, from the wife. If Pearl, *aleha ha-sholem*, couldn't get parked near an entrance and walk right into a store, *ai-ai-ai*, in a mall that smelled of Chanel Number 5 she wouldn't shop, for free! But for noshing, Pearl..."

Mr. Leo looked sort of doubtfully toward her statue, Henryetta thought, without saying *aleha ha-sholem*, which she reckoned must be Yiddish for "may she rest in peace" or somethin'. "The wife, she would shinny up a greased flag pole for a buttered bagel that didn't mix too much with shopping," he said. "And, you know, everybody's got to eat, I got to thinking. So..." So when Mr. Leo built the mall, he allowed no fast food on the street level and put all the food joints together in their own second level section, with a common dining area, fountains, trees, along with escalators and, to encourage people to go up there, the mall's public rest rooms, "'cause, you know, everybody's gotta go sometime. And that was the world's first food court," he said, "my little, you should pardon the expression, 'bastard,' conceived out of a fool's mistake."

This really was history, semi- worth bein' recorded and semi-interesting, Henryetta thought, as she jotted. It might even be a scoop, a Pulitzer Prize story no one had ever thought to ask about, but… "On television last year already," Mr. Leo said, "a big baldheaded *trombenik* from some 'Eastern Shore' got his face on the screen, so eager his horn to blow, and said <u>he</u> deserved the credit for the first food court—at a shopping mall in New Jersey already—and was also the 'mastermind' of a whole universe of other successful real estate projects, including Disney World already! The newswoman, to his big fat, grinning face, she told him he was a liar, and he…" Mr. Leo started laughing and talking in spurts. "He, the *trombenik,* said to her pretty face: 'I know, I know, but hear me out!'" And again, tears rolled down the old man's face. "He was just a salesman," he then said in a semi-serious tone, "and already he'd got to believe his own bullshit. Like a lot of people when they look back on their ordinary lives, he got to be, you should write down, conveniently 'forgetful'."

Henryetta, for the sake of correct journalism and history, felt she had to ask: "What happened to the other family business, the Fiddler's Green Cemetery that seems, maybe, not so…not so took care of as the mall?" Mr. Leo looked at her again like he thought she might be joking, or settin' up a joke for him to tell. "My son, he's got chronic high blonde pressure," he said, but in a way somber as an undertaker, so she didn't laugh. "My son," he said again, "my son, my trustee, my heir—he's a hopeless *schlemiel*—unlucky all the time already, and deserves to be. So desperate to hang on to this goddamned mall and that reeking food court, he lost a priceless treasure buried in the cemetery. My son is, excuse the Shakespeare expression, 'a base Indian who threw away a pearl richer than all his tribe.'"

On her way back home for lunch, Henryetta had a feeling that the ladies of Chelmsford Heights might be some surprised to read about the lowly beginin's of their town on its 50th anniversary, and then, as she was crossing Trolley Street... *This reporter got to thinking that the motive of the person or persons who stole the Weekly Weekender archives might have been more municipal than personal, not so much aimed at hiding anything exactly, but controlling and "varnishing" what got printed about Chelmsford Heights. And who would have had more concern about how the town got written up in The New York Times or USA Today than the ladies of the Lifestyle Alliance their own selves? They were the ones who came up with the anniversary project in the first place, and according to Mr. Harold Mixon — owner-and-publisher of the newspaper — the leading ladies of the Women's Alliance found out about the old Weekenders just a day or two before they were stolen, and may have been the only other persons to even know the archives existed. "I remember showing Mrs. Taliaferro and her friends all the boxes of materials we had to work with on a Friday," Mr. Mixon told this reporter yesterday. "On the following Monday, they were gone. And then...didn't think much about it at the time," he said later, "but now I recall that Mrs. Taliaferro seemed <u>pleased</u> when she told me that the Weekender's original owner, a man named Charlie Parker, had been found dead only the day before in Fiddler's Green Cemetery. So yes, I'm scared."*

*Quite possibly, therefor, the records documenting the Chelmsford Heights modern era have been buried somewhere by now in order for Mrs. Taliaferro and her bunch to put out their own bullshit that they want to believe is history. Despite the danger, this reporter intends to keep digging...*

Surprised and sad to see that the hearse was still parked in the driveway across Peach Street from her rent house, Henryetta was reminded to not get too carried away with her own ambition to win one of those Pulitzer Prizes. She parked her Checker, picked some flowers out of the garden of a house next door and…She decided it wasn't timely to intrude, what with someone's dead body still not hauled off, so she just put down the bouquet on the porch and said a little prayer that whoever was in there would have a place nicer than the rundown Fiddler's Green Cemetery to get laid.

# SIX

At the doorway of his management office, toward the Macy's end of the mall, Chester Grossman signed for personal receipt of a package wrapped in plain brown paper, then locked the door behind him before hurrying to his private bathroom. In front of a large vanity mirror mounted to a wall, he paused to reflect upon the brightly lit image of himself. Not bad for a man almost...still in his forties. Tall, handsome, impeccably groomed. Hair thinning a bit but still dark, with touches of what his stylist assured him was a subtle and perfectly natural raccoon mix. Face tanned, as always, and also as always, set off by a crispy white collar just as *Playman Manor* magazine prescribed. He flashed his dazzling smile, recently enhanced by a dentist trained by Vice-President Biden's personal enameler. People said he looked like a playboy, which he took as a compliment, and...To examine a blotch on the tip of his nose, Chester raised his horn rim dark glasses, but only for a moment. Bright light tended to make his eyes watery, and the surrounding areas puffy.

After stripping the wrapper from the just-arrived package, then opening a pink cardboard box and removing its contents, Chester turned his back to the mirror. He took off his tie, shirt, trousers and designer briefs. He would have preferred something in simple black or white, but had been put off by the gross images produced by his online search for men's foundation garments, and Fanny's Fashion Boutique carried Peek-a-Boo panty girdles only in pink. Women's sizes ran awfully small, he thought, struggling to get into the Super-Duper Maxi Model, but…Strapped in, but unable to fully bend over, Chester again struggled to to get into his roomy man-sized pants. Finally re-dressed, he turned to again look at himself in the mirror. Not too bad for a man whose old high school debate club injury—to his shoulder—made regular exercise difficult to maintain. Not bad at all, he thought, as he turned off the vanity light and set out from his office for a secret rendezvous in a secluded corner of the mall.

As effectively the owner of Chelmsford Heights Mall, often referred to as the community's "high temple"—sort of like its Masonic Lodge, in Chester's mind—he enjoyed the social trappings of his position, and took pride in being seen outside the mall as landlord and sort of "Masonic Worshipful Master" of the upscale merchants that gave to the people of Chelmsford Heights their very reason to live. On the other hand, as somewhat ineffectively the mall's general manager, responsible for day-to-day operations and maintenance of the property developed years ago by his father, Chester dreaded most other aspects of his job, in particular the seeing-and-being-seen ritual of patrolling the shopping center's covered and enclosed "street." While others who strolled Rodeo Drive beheld only the beauty of its terrazzo pavement, the grandeur of its faux Greek columns, the public art such as the taxidermy pieces in the Prancing Peacocks Court that he now passed, and the elegance of mall storefronts, Chester registered only floor cracks, water damage from skylight leaks, the prying eyes of the prancing peacocks and, behind painted drywall facades, deferred maintenance that would cost more to address than demolition and reconstruction of the entire aging building. While shoppers were charmed by the fawning attention of store owners and managers who catered to their every whim and... "Chester! Chester!" came a familiar shrill voice, right on cue.

Unable to hurry past the ambush or fully twist his girdled hips and torso to partially deflect the attack, Chester made a tight half circle and absorbed a full frontal assault by Sherry Cavanaugh, proprietor of Dear John's greeting card store. "Chester!" the middle-aged woman again shouted, now from close range, out of breath and visibly sweating. "It's late June already, Chester, the wedding season's almost gone, and my store, it's like a Turkish bath in there. Envelopes are sealing up themselves, on the racks, empty as bridal altar promises. Chester, you gotta do something about the air conditioning! Please, I'm begging you, do something!" Though knowing the mission would be futile, Chester followed Sherry back to her store. Inside the "bath house," like two old goats looking at a new gate, they blankly stared at a recently installed wall-mounted thermostat set at seventy-two degrees.

"Must be another faulty unit," Chester said. "We'll order a new one and..."

"Faulty already," said Sherry Cavanaugh, grabbing the gadget in obvious anger and jerking. "Hmmm," said Chester, now that it was obvious that the violently unmounted empty plastic box had never had any connection to a no doubt worn out HVAC unit on the mall roof. The ruse was one of his father's standard management techniques, passed down to a longtime chief of mall maintenance. "Sherry, you gotta keep your doors open to avoid build-up of hot air," he said, maneuvering himself toward the doors. "Open?" he heard the unhappy tenant say from behind him. "It's early morning, for cryin' out loud. You want me to keep the doors open <u>all</u> <u>night</u>? It's you with the hot air, Chester, you're a disgrace to your father's good name!"

That parting shot in the back was uncalled for, Chester thought, as he continued on his way, and one of these days might not go unanswered. Dear John's was another hopelessly outdated store from Leo's days in charge, but Sherry Cavanaugh's longterm lease would finally expire at the end of the year and the space might just go—as-is, to be refurbished and re-equipped by tenant—to a retailer with a new, exciting merchandising concept such as his wife, Shelley, longed for. She had been nagging him to hire a new leasing broker who would…Through the wide-open doors of Kevin's Koins & Kollectibles, Chester saw another distressed store owner come from behind a counter. Kevin Kelley did not attack him, however—he slunk through a back door into a storage room—and neither did Chester go after the tenant for almost a full year of unpaid back rent. His former fraternity brother, a stock broker his whole adult life, had fallen on hard times, and had come up with the idea of opening KKK's in the mall to sell-off inherited coins and stamps collections. It wasn't working, and the situation had become embarrassing for both of them. Kevin just lacked the knack for retail, it seemed. Maybe he could move Sherry into the over-sized, fairly cool space with KKK for the remainder of summer, Chester thought, as he continued to walk the gauntlet. Sometimes the hunter, sometimes the…

No, he was always the prey when he marched down the mall, Chester admitted to himself. Kevin Kelley had taken advantage of their friendship and…He again veered to avoid another possible tenant encounter—this time with the manager of one of the women's apparel chain stores that were the heart and soul of the mall: the main source of its income stream and upscale image. Banana Republic was one of the charter members of a sort of "club" of specialty stores of similar taste level that also included Abercrombie & Fitch, J. Jill, Ralph Lauren, J. Crew, Coach etcetera, and even more upscale A/X Armani Exchange, Barney's New York, Betsey Johnson, Hugo Boss, Louis Viutton, Tiffany and that bunch. He'd been waiting for weeks for Banana Republic's corporate headquarters to either accept or not a lease renewal at desperately needed higher rent but, in his present fragile state of mind, couldn't bear to face possible rejection by "the club."

At the mall's center court in front of Miss Margaret's of Chelmsford Heights, a high-end women's and girls' apparel store on two floors, Chester paused to watch workmen begin installation of the runway for this Saturday's fashion show of a new retro line of "Princess to Di 4" outfits. When completed, the red carpet would extend three-hundred feet, the length of a football field, to and past the Prancing Peacocks Court all the way to Macy's. Hundreds of dressed-up women from the Chelmsford Heights area and beyond would come to see and be seen. Dozens would inevitably act surprised to learn from a newspaper photographer that they had wandered onto the models' scarlet path, even though *Caught on the Runway* was a popular monthly photo feature of the *Weekly Weekender.* Hopefully stores along the way, maybe even Dear John's and KKK would benefit from the fashion show shopper traffic and have decent sales volumes. Stores in the opposite direction, with one exception—hopeless, Chester thought, as he entered the twilight zone of outdated zombie stores that his father—mainly—had put in.

Looking across the Flying Flamingos Court reflecting pool, he made a mental note to install taller potted bushes to better screen Leo's unsightly...Uh oh, he'd been spotted by the mall's most unlikable tenant, "Biggie" Friedman. From inside his store the men's shoe merchant was looking at him over a shoulder, disengaging himself from a customer, no doubt intent on badgering his landlord for a lease renewal for the large space a few doors down from Fanny's Fashion Boutique. Friedman had occupied the premises for fifteen contentious years, and though his lease had expired almost a year ago, Chester had allowed him to continue in business since then as a "tenant-at-will" on a month-to-month basis. He hadn't had the heart to kick Biggie out. The obnoxiously aggressive little schmuck had begun to generate exceptionally high sales, and currently paid the highest per-square-foot rent of any tenant in Chelmsford Heights Mall, despite the poor location of his store — Big Dicks Footwear.

Since becoming the area's exclusive outlet for the Longfellow Shoes brand two years ago, Biggie's store had been on the so-called "cutting edge" of new retail merchandising, Chester had to admit, at least in the sense that no other chain had yet come out with a watered down version of its concept: over-sized men's shoes with inflatable toe inserts for "better balance." But Biggie himself — only about 5' 7" or so in height, with probably only a size 6 foot — was his own advertising spokesman, and that was a problem. Thanks to his nightly TV ads, his baldheaded, bug-eyed visage was becoming virtually "the face" of Chelmsford Heights Mall, his message a blot on the town's image and reputation for good taste. "Hey, guys, what's the first thing a woman notices about a man?" he would ask, to start each spiel for that week's special — usually a pair of shoes made of the skin of some exotic reptile, though last week his "Blind Date Icebreaker Special" featured huge boots made of walrus hide. "Make a <u>big</u>

impression, fellas," he would say at the end of each spiel, "with Big Dick Shoes, they're (wink) Longfellows!" Chester had taken him to small claims court on multiple occasions, but…Now here he came, tromping from his store into the mall in snowshoe-size brown-and-black saddle oxfords, waggling a finger. "Chester," he said, "where's my new lease? I want to make improvements to my store, but without a guarantee…"

"We've already been through this, Morris," Chester said, "until you conform…"

"My name's now 'Richard,'" Friedman said, "long for 'Dick'. I had it changed, so I could…"

"Yes, I know, so you could re-name your store and put up that sign. But your old lease says you are Morris Friedman, doing business as Biggie's Fine Footwear for Men, and…"

"Chester, what's with you and the sign, for cryin' out loud? The judge said that in my own legal name I could…"

"You told the judge your new name was Richard. If she'd known you were a Dick, she would have…At the very least, she would have required you to sign yourself with an apostrophe 's', as simply 'Big Dick's Shoes'."

"With a what?! What is it with you old guard Heightsters?" Biggie said, looking down at Chester's almost size 10 custom made wing-tip tassel loafers from London. "Puffing yourself up with 'airs', you make yourselves look small. C'mon into the store, Chester," Biggie said, "let me put you in a pair of 'White Snake16's', at my cost. They'll enlarge your whole opinion of yourself, and as for the ladies…Shoes are the first thing a woman notices about a man. Big shoes, big…"

"So I hear, nightly," said Chester, "but…Morris, I may as well tell you now. I'm going to make some major changes to the mall. In fact, I have already started working with a brilliant architect, Bruno Camaleonte, to draw up…"

"Bruno? He's a customer," Friedman said. "An 18 triple D. Ask him how he likes the 'Swinging Big Dick' golf shoes I put on him. Highest quality lizard, they'll last a lifetime, and double the length of your driver."

Though tempted to try on a pair, Chester stood firm, and told Biggie he should start looking for new store space in some other location. The little shoe merchant wailed that he'd just signed up to carry a new line of men's briefs called "Jockey Socks," which sealed his fate in Chester's mind. "Fanny's Boutique carries padded bras and padded panty girdles," the insufferable tenant-at-will argued, which gave Chester reason to pause, though not to reconsider what to do about Big Dick Footwear. In the Fanny Super-Duper Maxi-Model he wore, his trousers did feel a bit "padded," now that he thought about it. Could there have been a mistake with his order? "You're not the man your father was, Chester," Friedman said, turning away with a wave of disgust; then over his shoulder: "Leo, he got it, sex sells, but you, Chester, you're an uptight-nik."

Feeling even more exposed to the slings and arrows of seeing and being seen on mall patrol, Chester hurried toward… "Well, well, well, if it's not Chelmsford Heights' own cock-o'-the-walk, back to struttin' his stuff," said Fanny O'Brien, come from her boutique to block his escape from duty. "Didn't I try to tell you, Chester? A man, 'specially one your age, is gonna get more satisfaction from a butterball than a fryer." He had only a vague idea about what the chubby middle-aged woman was talking about. "What's it been," she said, "six or seven years with that little blonde guinea hen, for you to figure out a man needs some cushion-for-the-pushin'?"

"Now, cut that out, Fanny," he said. "I'm a happily married man, and I intend to stay that way this time."

"Uh huh," she said. "I suppose you and that skinny wife you're so happy with are gonna get into that crotchless Peek-a-Boo French underwear <u>together</u> for this weekend's fashion show—and go at it like two horny possums in a gunny sack. Don't get 'caught on the runway,' Chester, not again."

Too mortified to explain the…the orthopedic background of what had been advertised as a confidential transaction by mail, as well as unable to breathe—and feeling that his face had turned from tan to red—Chester darted into a service corridor. At the end of the hallway, inside a semi-refrigerated garbage room, he ripped off his jacket, tie and shirt, dropped his pants to the littered concrete floor, and tore at the velcro straps of the damned Peek-a-Boo Super-Duper Maxi Model. He'd only wanted to look his best for accidentally bumping into Shelley at *Chez de Crepes* and…The room's overhead light went out. Chester froze. "Who's there?" he yelled, in a voice that came out squeakier than he would have liked.

"No, that's what Mr. X. says," came a deep-throated reply. "And it's…Who <u>goes</u> there?"

"Dad-gum-it! Turn the light back on," Chester answered, feeling both relieved and annoyed, as well as a little chilly. But…

"Who goes there?" the deep voice asked. "Fee-fi-fo-fum!"

"Oh, alright," Chester yelled. "An Englishman, I mean a bloody Englishman goes there. Now turn on the light and come over here. Someone might overhear us if we keep shouting at each other."

"Mr. X can't risk being seen," said the voice of the other man, well known to Chester as a Chelmsford Heights policeman who, for discreet encounters such as this, stubbornly referred to himself by alias—always in the third person—as Mr. X, and to Chester as Mr. O. "Mr. X thinks he may have been spotted casing the joint," the off-duty cop said. "It's dangerous out there and"—the now low voice came from close enough by that "Mr. O" could smell that "Mr. X" had recently smoked a cigarette—"at least one other hired gun is stalking the lady in question."

""Someone else is after her?" said Chester, alarmed. "We need to make our move, <u>now</u>!"

"Easy for Mr. O to say," came the whispered reply. "Mr. X needs more information about where she's likely to be holed up"

"I don't have any more. I've given you…"

"…and more money for expenses. Mr. X is going to have to bring in some muscle. Know what I mean? She's gonna be a real bitch to get at, it's gonna to be a dirty job."

"I've told you already, I don't want anyone else to know about this…this job. Not even your wife, no matter how cold blooded you say she is. Women blab, I always end up on the front page of the *Weekender*. And no 'muscle.' I don't want her…roughed up."

"She won't feel a thing."

"I mean it. Mr. O means it. She's not to be hurt!"

"Not a problem. But on his own, Mr. X would have to give up his bowling night, and weekends, so it'll be overtime, you know. And if you want me to be gentle with her…"

Chester reached for his wallet, only to be reminded he was bare-assed naked, except for his socks and almost size 10 shoes that somehow made his feet feel small in the semi-refrigerated air. "Mr. O will stash extra funds in the usual place," he said. "And, uh, better for Mr. X not to turn on the light as he leaves. Too dangerous that…that Mr. O might see you, or be seen."

"No problem."

"And to repeat," said Chester: "as I've told you before, be gentle with her. She was the only woman…She was my mother, for cryin' out loud, the only woman who sort of loved Mr. O 'til…'til another woman took her place."

# SEVEN

Chief O'Connor sat at her desk in police headquarters, proof-reading a summary police blotter. The weekly task had become more tedious and time consuming since this year's alternate naming of most of the town's avenues, boulevards, courts, drives, lanes, places and ways. She had complained, not about the clerical burden, but about the dangerous effect of slower police response time to crimes in progress and other emergencies. Neither she nor anyone else in the police and fire departments could speak or understand pronunciation of French words and...Bulldog sighed. Wholesale changes in progress to the town's architectural style were difficult enough to follow. Just by looking, she was no longer absolutely sure who belonged in each residence and who might be an intruder. During the past few years countless Chelmsford Heights houses—originally copied from ye olde English countryside, according to local lore—had been torn down and replaced, or stripped and "re-imagined," most "in the manner of the South of France," according to what she'd read—their brick veneers and gabled roofs discarded in favor of faux stone and "hipped" slate roofs. And to further enhance a "Provencale ambience," as well as demonstrate cultural diversity, street names...Bulldog again sighed, and returned to proof-reading the blotter report:

*On June 18: Officer on routine patrol noticed a suspicious subject in the area of Kent Mews/Rue de Avignon and Viceroy Lane/LeRoi Soleil. Officer made contact with the subject and was advised the subject was a resident of CH, out walking.*

*On June 18: Officer responded to call reporting that a resident heard noise of shattering dishes inside adjacent house on Pall Mall Place/Arles Avenue. Officer was advised by house occupants that all was normal.*

*On June 18: Officer on routine patrol noticed suspicious subject in the area of Kent Mews/Rue de Avignon and Viceroy Lane/LeRoi Soleil. Officer made contact with the subject and was advised the subject was still a resident of CH, and still out walking.*

The chief paused to consider her blotter entry. This wasn't an official police department document that couldn't be altered, it was only an informal "eyes only" summary for Mrs. Taliaferro, the town's mayoress. To uphold fear and respect for law enforcement in Chelmsford Heights, Her Honoress herself would likely delete or even add some detail before passing on the report to the *Weekly Weekender* for publication. Hells bells, three years or so ago, Chief Bulldog had been surprised to see a large photo of her own self on the front page of the local newspaper, headlined WELCOME TO CHELMSFORD HEIGHTS, and more surprised to read that with the newly issued automatic weapon pictured in her hands, she had shot and killed a door-to-door solicitor in the front lawn of a house on what was then plain ol' Kools Lite Lane. "Let this be a warning to others," she was quoted as having said. "The Heights are for residents only."

She had inquired about the absence of a body for her to pay her respects and regrets to, but… "The story was 'planted,'" Mrs. Taliaferro had explained. "I felt we had to set an example <u>before</u> you actually used your new toy on a resident who was out walking." Chief Bulldog deleted two previous entries for her June 18 patrol and went back to proof reading:

*On June 18: Officers were dispatched to a residence on Viceroy Lane/LeRoi Soleil in response to complaint of domestic violence. No one came to the door, but officers heard dogs barking inside the house, so returned to base.*

*On June 20: Officer on routine patrol noticed a suspicious suspect carrying a suspicious bag at the corner of Parliament Circle/St. Trophine. After determining subject was not a resident, officer escorted subject out of CH to his place of employment at a nearby post office.*

*On June 20: Officer on routine patrol noticed a suspicious subject in the area of Kent Mews/Rue de Avignon and Viceroy Lane/LeRoi Soleil. Officer made contact with subject who maintained she was still…* Chief Bulldog made a final edit to the blotter, got up from her desk and walked from the police department toward the front of ye olde town hall. In a kitchen area, where the J.C. Penney crapper used to be located, she found a leftover mud ball, poured a cup of forty-weight for herself, and reviewed bulletin board postings:

**NOTICE OF PENDING ORDINANCE:** *By enactment of this OrdinanceCH-57329, all duly licensed, contracted and bonded workmen engaged to make approved improvements to existing residences or erect new structures or mow lawns shall first report to the Building Department on each day of work to obtain approval of their apparel and general appearance. Without such approval no workmen shall be allowed to dig, hammer, paint…*

# 4TH OF JULY
# SCHEDULE & POLICE SECURITY ASSIGNMENTS

| | |
|---|---|
| 0600 hrs. | Full Force muster in CHPD parking lot |
| 0700 hrs. | End of coffee & donut service |
| | Latrine break in twos |
| 0800 hrs. | Deployment of Force: |
| 1000 hrs. | Return to Base for Coffee Break |
| 1100 hrs. | Escort "Big Enchilada" * to Hall of Fame |
| 1200 hrs. | Salute to Unknown Resident * ** |
| 1300 hrs. | Start of Parade |
| 1400 hrs. | Coffee Break at CHPD |
| 1500 hrs. | Redeployment to Posts |
| 1600 hrs. | Speech by "Big Enchilada" * |
| 1800 hrs. | Salute to Known Residents*** |
| 1900 hrs. | Dismissal from Duty |
| 2000 hrs. | Picnic & Beer     Residents Only |
| 2100 hrs. | Fireworks & More Beer *     Full Force Off-Duty |

*Need to know only. **One gun/21 shots. *** 2 guns/ full magazines.

Satisfied with arrangements for the upcoming 4th of July, Chief O'Connor turned her attention to the next posted bulletin: VOLUNTEERS WANTED FOR HONORARY DUTY... "Hey, Bulldog, what's cookin'?" said the voice of a subordinate officer who'd come up beside her. "You look like you got a whiff of somethin' bad."

"Maybe yes, maybe no," she replied, after turning to face the fellow cop. "Looks like we might have a smoker in mall truck dock number four. Marlboro man, possibly."

"Oh yeah?" he said. "I didn't see nothin' about it on the blotter."

"Off the record," she explained. "Covert operation, 'need to know' classified for the time being."

"No shit! You got Mr. X workin' undercover inside the freakin' mall? Sumbitch! You got <u>some</u> balls, Bulldog."

"Keep that on the q.t., can't risk it leaking to the *Weekender* snoops," she said, before continuing on her way to the ye olde town hall mail room. Bulldog was surprised, not that no one had volunteered for honorary duty, but that the mayoress had made the request—citing for the first time ever, "municipal budgetary considerations." As an army vet herself, she was in favor of Mrs. Taliaferro's proposal for posting a round-the-clock uniformed guard at the new Hall of Fame Columbarium. At recent dedication ceremonies for the facility, a jar of nuts and bolts had been put in one of its niches—sort of like an "unknown soldier"—to honor fallen Chelmsford Heightsters still left behind enemy lines in Fiddler's Green Cemetery. If not for the requirement imposed by a rogue faction of the Women's Alliance—sponsored by Chester Grossman's wife but also opposed by Mrs. Taliaferro—that the honor guard had to wear the uniform of an apparently famous Frenchman named "John Darme," Bulldog herself might have volunteered to stand beside the niched jar for a four-hour shift from time to time. But to serve at no pay was too much to ask of overworked off-duty rank-and-file police officers and firemen.

After depositing the summary police blotter in the mayoress' mail slot, Chief O'Connor lingered at the sliding glass front door of ye olde town hall, looking with longing into the mall. She missed the duty and the good times she'd had working the Rodeo Drive beat—her chats along the way with Mr. Leo Grossman and his sub-tenants, the variety of snacks available to her in the second-level food court, the armed security she'd personally provided to keep unknown overweight wannabe models off the red runway during mall fashion shows. And she worried about what dirty deeds were even now afoot on Chester Grossman's unsecured premises that threatened the lives and lifestyle of innocent Chelmsford Heights shoppers. The mayoress had said she thought a town-wide roll call to check for missing residents was not called for, based on lack of conclusive evidence of rampant body snatching. But Mrs. Taliaferro was an untrained civilian, not aware that toleration of, say, truck dock smoking inevitably led to sloppy food court maintenance, then to shoppers spitting on the floor and…maybe shoplifting, maybe even…Hells bells, rumors of declining mall sales and town sales taxes were probably true, and no wonder!

A large cuckoo clock on the wall above her announced an hour of decision, clear as a dog whistle to Bulldog's trained ears. In reflexive answer to the call to duty, she charged into the mall, past the *Weekly Weekender* office and Mr. Leo's landscaped patio, around the Flying Flamingos reflecting pool, and into a service corridor leading to truck dock number four. At a metal door, she unholstered her gun with one hand, a flashlight with the other, then entered a semi-darkened, semi-refrigerated room, but…The air was polluted by odors of food court garbage and Bulldog was unable to immediately detect any tell-tale trace of Marlboro cigarette smoking. She scanned the littered floor with her flashlight beam and… "Hello," she muttered to herself, "what have we here?" At her feet, lying in a bed of wilted lettuce leaves and partially covered by some sliced onions and a crouton or two, a woman's pink panty girdle—coupled with the faint smell of *Playman* after-shave cologne—proved someone had recently been…And yes, the body of that person was nowhere about. After poking at the conclusive evidence with the tip of her flashlight, she picked up the large foul underthing and—just as a bright overhead light came on—Bulldog detected that it was a Super-Duper Maxi Model and <u>crotchless</u>!

"Chief O'Connor," said a voice from behind her, "could you please explain to me what's been goin' on around here?"

# EIGHT

At about quarter-to-four, Phoebe Taliaferro-Dugan, otherwise known as Mrs. Henry Taliaferro-Dugan and to family and friends as "Tutu," was aflutter with anxiety. She'd dared to add a few subtle French touches to her party arrangements and now worried…Her mother, *grande dame* of old-line Chelmsford Heights society—and Tutu too—were currently at odds with a somewhat younger group within the Women's Lifestyle Alliance sometimes referred to as the "French faction," and…And now it appeared to Tutu that poison being sprayed around the terrace of her Pall Mall Place/*St. Trophine* home might be doing more harm than good. Fowl of every common feather continued to perch on and around her priceless collection of ceramic birds arrayed on bistro tables covered with elegant *Pierre Deux* fabrics. Shrill squawks from agitated doves—bound up in mesh bags hanging from trees—filled the air, along with bits of downy fluff, as hawks circled overhead in descending loops. Her *Tea-4:00-Tutu* affair to officially announce pending certification of a Chelmsford Heights Chapter of Birds & Bird Lovers Unlimited was in danger of not coming off as another "too, too perfect" event such as she was known for staging. And a photographer from the *Weekly Weekender* had not arrived on time to capture the fleeting beauty of the floral-and-fruits buffet centerpiece now being cleaned of bird droppings by one of the catering staff from Gregory's Gourmet Good-Eats & Company.

Phoebe glanced at a bejeweled watch on her fleshy wrist. The dramatic climax she'd planned for the conclusion of today's *le the'* would have to be moved up, she realized, maybe to the very beginning, and that would ruin... "Professor Lehough has arrived," said a liveried member of Chef Gregory's staff, who snickered, then added, "and a Miss 'Henryetta Something' from the newspaper, who wants you to know that her name is spelled with..." "Hurry!" Phoebe commanded, before flying outside to the buffet centerpiece. "Stand here!" she said to the rumpled-looking professor who had shuffled after her onto the terrace. "And <u>yew</u>," she said, pointing a pudgy, pink-nailed finger at the *Weekender* photographer named...whatever, "take the pictures from over there, slightly to my left. And <u>do</u> <u>not</u> miss the *coup d' gras* this time!"

After a few seconds—satisfied with the photo-op set-up—for the benefit of the gardeners assembled off-camera, Tutu shouted, "Thank you, Professor, for your most informative and entertaining remarks about our fine feathered friends and lovers." And on cue—she gazing upward, Professor Lehough beside her, the oddly-named *Weekender* photographer clicking a camera—dozens of frightened doves, released from captivity, flew into the air and—to Tutu's distress, into the house.

"Oh my gawd, Tutu, you've outdone yourself again," said the leader of a dressed-up gaggle of age forty-something women who sashayed in for tea. "Oh my gawd, Tutu," agreed each and every one of the two dozen others who followed. But then, her mother—also named Phoebe but known to family and friends as "Mumu"…"For cryin' out loud, Phoebe, get these horrid birds out of here," big Phoebe said, looking unusually hot-and-bothered in a loose-fitting flowered dress. "And close the damned doors," added one of the ladies. "It's hotter than whoopee-in-woolens outside."

With the doves finally gone—and given that the Birds & Bird Lovers Unlimited accreditation, now possibly in jeopardy, was only one of countless things planned for observance of Chelmsford Heights' 50th anniversary celebration, and a minor one at that—the professor, along with what would have been his no doubt informative and possibly entertaining remarks, were scratched from the tea party agenda, along with an exchange of civic award plaques between Phoebe and…whomever. Instead, attention focused, as usual, on Tutu's mother, the *grande dame*. "I've asked Chester to face us," she announced to the circle of Women's Alliance ladies gathered around her. "He's got no spine, as everyone knows," she said, "but may still be enough enthralled with that skinny wife of his to show up and try to sell that cockeyed so-called 'idea' of hers for what—and who—would best represent our upscale lifestyle, and no less important"—she looked with dubious expression at the girl in jeans and tee-shirt from the *Weekly Weekender*—"what images of what and who would be most fitting for publication in *The New York Times* or *USA Today*."

Mumu paused and looked at the girl again, no doubt recalling how vicious a free press could be, Phoebe thought. What's-Her-Name—camera hanging from her neck, notebook and pencil in hand—then sidled up beside her. "Do you correctly spell your name as T-o-t-o," she asked, "or T-o-o-t-o-o…And what about 'Taliaferro'…I don't read Italian, so I'm not sure…"

"It's olde English, pronounced 'Tolliver,'"Tutu answered,"and only my intimate friends call me…" "Just refer to my daughter as Mrs. Phoebe Taliaferro-Dugan," said her mother, staring at the new *Weekender* reporter with a look of unamused appraisal. "That's 'Dugan' with a 'u', my dear, and before you ask, yes, same as 'Mumu'—M-u-m-u, as in this dress I'm wearing—but that's not for you to mention."

As a burst laughter came from the kitchen and…Phoebe was again set aflutter when Chester Grossman walked into her living room from the entry hall. "How do, How do, How do," he said, throwing kisses into the air like confetti as he made his way through her circle of friends and, alas, past her puckered lips with nary a glance. "Mu - mu - mu - mu," he said, arms open wide enough to encompass all outdoors for delivery of a hug to his once-prospective mother-in law, "you look blooming lovely as the whole Lord Chelmsford Park in that flowery dress, and twice as…"

"Save the bon bons for that underfed wife of yours, Chester," Mumu said, rudely pushing past his offered embrace to the center of a reconfigured circle of the women present. "What's it to be, Chesty," she then said, after turning around to face him. "Are you going to march like a man with the old guard of the Lifestyle Alliance, or pussy-foot down the runway in a dress?"

"Now, now, Mumu," he said, "and girls," he added with a glance in obviously desperate search of potential allies. "I'm sure yours and Shelley's conflicting…ah, different ideas…are just a tempest in a tea…What if it rains on the day of the big blow-out? Have you considered that very strong possibility? Ladies,"he said, searching the circle again, "think of your fifteth anniversary hair-dos."

At issue was whether culmination of the town's anniversary festivities would be a traditional residents-only parade from Lord Chelmsford Park to a catered picnic on country club grounds, or a so-called "*tres chic*" residents-only candlelit dinner dance and fashion show in the mall. The so-called old guard, comprised of first, second and third generations of Chelmsford Heights women, led by Mumu—and Tutu as nominal Co-Chairlady—favored the former option that would feature them, together with children and grandchildren. The somewhat younger, and distinctly slimmer so-called French faction, led by Chester's current wife, Shelley—also a Co-Chairlady—were determined to display what they called a more "active contemporary lifestyle," in keeping with which they themselves—after running something called a 5K—would cook an organic gourmet dinner, themselves model the most so-called "with-it" lifestyle fashion apparel, then dine and dance 'til dawn with friends and family, *sans* pesky children.

"...hail, possibly tornados," Chester continued. "Or—it will be mid-July, don't forget, so it'll be hotter than..."

"No hotter than inside the mall, you cheapskate," said Mumu. "And the fireworks—they've been paid for and <u>will</u> be shot off, indoors or out!"

"Not outside if it rains, Mumu, not if it rains on your parade!"

"Chester, you're a hopeless fool. We haven't had rain in July since Pap was a pup."

"And I'm not going to model any of Shelley's skimpy dresses for you," said Tutu. "I...I...I've got a swollen sprained ankle that won't be well by then."

"I'm not cookin' any 'organic' food, I'll tell you that right now," said another of the old guard. "My Dougie and the kids won't eat anything that's been fed or fertilized with manure. They like fried chicken."

"And what about the Proud Pets Parade?" said another. "We always do it in the mall and…I'm not going to have my boy, Roy, carrying a parakeet cage outdoors in July rain, or heat. And think of the reptiles, the turtles, the…"

"Hire the little boy a pet-walker like everybody else," Chester answered. "Let little, er, Roy play with the other kids at the club pool. It'll likely be hot as a featherbed in a honeymoon hotel in late…"

"My little Roy's not a 'little boy,' he's almost twenty-one and he's been lookin' forward to…"

"You seem to forget, Chester: Tutu is also co-chair of the big Celebration Committee, and senior," said Mumu, "as well as Parade Marshallene!"

"Marshallene?"

"She will not be called a French 'ette' of any kind," Phoebe's mother said, to which Phoebe herself added that she would not "lead a march down that narrow red carpet! I'm too, too…"

In the midst of her almost tearful confession, noticing that the *Weekender* reporter was jotting down in her notebook what had to be way more than just names of those present and what they were wearing, Phoebe caught the girl's attention with the wave of one "swollen" hand and dismissed her with a jerk of her thumb. As the girl opened a door to the kitchen to exit, out came another burst of laughter, including the distinctive shrill squeal of Phoebe's daughter, "Kuku," home from college for the summer and supposedly… "Oh my gawd, it's yew!" she heard Kuku say before the door closed.

Still distracted about what on earth her daughter could be doing in the kitchen with the hired help, Phoebe then heard

Chester say that he'd wanted something to be a surprise, but…
With his arms in the air as if to surrender to her, alas, again…
"I…I mean the mall merchants association," he continued,
"because Shelley's…because this community event is so…'about'
the mall…well, I'll foot the entire cost and justify it to the
merchants by using the occasion to make a very, very special
announcement of a coming blessed event that will…"

"Oh no!" Phoebe blurted, stunned and dismayed to think
Shelley Grossman was to be the mother of Chester's child. "Oh
yes!" said her mother, which was even more stunning. "Chester,
you've got yourself a deal," Mumu said, "subject to working out
the details, we'll have the big anniversary blow-out in our beloved
upscale mall." She then took Phoebe aside. "About that nosy girl
from the *Weekender*," she said, "she's flying blind, obviously with
no clue about our upsacale lifestyle, and no way to learn about
us. We're going to have to keep an eye on her, and make sure
we know and approve of what she writes on her own before it's
published. Let's not forget, Phoebe, how vicious an unmonitored
press can be."

# NINE

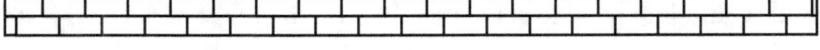

At a computer in the *Weekly Weekender* office, Henryetta reviewed her snapshots and captions under a header:

TEA - 4:00 - MRS. PHOEBE TALIAFERRO - DUGAN to BENEFIT UNLIMITED BIRDS & LOVERS:

*Mrs. Taliaferro - Dugan (shown here on left) welcomes birds into her house, as Professor Lehough (shown here on right) looks down at something they must have dropped on his shoes.*

*Mrs. Taliaferro - Dugan (shown here from behind) shoos birds out of her house with a broom, as Professor Lehough (shown on his knees) tries to save one of them with artificial respiration.*

*Mrs. Mumu Taliaferro (shown in an unmentionable dress) samples fruit salad at the tea party, and a ham sandwich, as Chef Gregory (in background) enjoys a good laugh.*

*Mr. Chester Grossman (shown backed against a wall) listens to Mrs. Mumu Taliaferro tell how the cow ate the cabbage. That's Mrs. Taliaferro - Dugan's hand (shown there on the left) clinging to Mr. Grossman's arm.*

*Miss Phoebe "Kuku" Taliaferro - Dugan, home from the Tri Phi Phi sorority house in Norman for the summer, hugs Chef Gregory in the kitchen from behind (with one hand down the front of his pants), as he laughs and sprinkles sweat and hair into fruit salad.*

Henryetta put those and other submissions into a file for publication this weekend, and got up from the table. The last one was a dirty trick on Kuku, she knew, but Mr. Harold would review it along with the others for correct journalism, and if it did get put in the paper—well, Kuku started the friction between 'em, and would just have to set on the blister, she reckoned. Henryetta had sort of thought there was somethin' familiar about one of the voices coming out of the kitchen, laughing at her 'cause she didn't know olde English from Italian, and when Mrs. Taliaferro-Dugan sent her in there to take pictures…Kuku and the other Tri Phi Phi girls down at OU had been making fun of her all along, Henryetta now knew, maybe because of her grammar—when she got carried away about somethin' she tended to…Or maybe they didn't think she amounted to much because of her crooked front tooth, or her clothes, she figured. So she was gonna take up Mr. Harold on his merciful offer, and charge up some new outfits at the Miss Margaret's store in the mall, then go see a dentist about gettin' a brace put on to keep herself from smilin' so much.

Inside Miss Margaret's store, a woman with short black hair looked her up and down like an insurance company adjuster—shaking her head and goin' tsk, tsk— about to declare a total crop failure. "She should be stuffed and put in a Ripley's Believe It - or - Not museum," she said to a co-salesman, a young fella also wearin' nothing but black clothes and silver jewelry. Their name tags said she went by "Amanda," him by "Andy," and to Henryetta they looked like they'd been mixed in the same bowl. "She's 'earthy' but clean," he said. "Eyes blue as cornflowers, hair like sun-bleached strawberries, thick as weeds but soft as corn silk. And the tooth…"

"A little too earthy, quite a lot too 'corny'," said the woman, "and yes, the tooth…"

"To die for," said Andy. "Where did you have it done, Miss…?"

"Just call me Henryetta," Henryetta said, "spelled with a 'y' 'cause I was named after the town where…"

"She's perfect," the Andy man said, after half-circling her. "Absolutely perfect," the Amanda woman agreed. "She needs a complete Chelmsford Heights make over."

Not exactly knowing what a "make over" was, Henryetta told Amanda she came in just to get a fresh set of work clothes and maybe some dress-up shoes. "Good," said Amanda, "we got a truckload of fresh work clothes in today, and shoes. Now, go behind the curtain and say good-bye to everything you have on."

"I'll take the jeans as a trade-in," Andy said. "Kay Kay is looking for something *declasse*, and the John Deere patch on the fanny is priceless."

Henryetta felt like she had to go along for the sake of Mr. Harold, and for the sake of her own career too. So she put on the little ol' oldtime feed-sack print dress handed in to her and came out from behind the curtain feeling girlish as… "OMG!" Andy said. "Mandy, she's a boy! Small up top, no hips at all, a tush to die for."

"Yes," said Amanda, looking at her with a hand up at her chin, like she was sizing up a roaster for Sunday supper and wasn't decided whether to wring her neck or let her fatten up for a week or so. "She's a perfect misfit. Let's try to fix her."

Putting on and taking off clothes for the next hour, Henryetta had never seen or heard such a fuss. Amanda wanted a bunch of head-to-toe dark outfits for her, and said they would make her look "longer and a little bit chic." Andy disagreed and kept putting her in light colors, 'cause of her own fairness, he said. Then Amanda made her try on some shoes she called "five-inch wedge escadrilles like Shelley Grossman wears," but Andy practically yanked 'em off her feet after seeing her walk "like Shelley, with mincing steps of, uh, a more 'mature' preying cat." He put her in some one-inch "kitten heels," which he argued were better suited for "a contemporary professional lifestyle." There were no price tags on anything, Henryetta noticed. "They're tacky," Amanda said, and Andy agreed it was "crass to monetize lifestyle."

About the only other thing the two of them agreed on was that her slightly crooked front tooth was her best feature, which was a mercy to Henryetta.

But then, in the store beauty parlor, they got back to fussin' like sisters—Amanda on one side of the chair, Andy on the other, each tellin' the licensed cosmetologists how they ought to be doin' their jobs. Henryetta knew the beauticians were bridlin' at all the instruction, 'cause she was the daughter of one her own self—Wynona Sue, her mother, had worked for years at the Best Little Hair House in Henryetta before recently sailin' off from Catoosa to Acapulco on the *S.S. Barge* to get married again, by and to the captain of the ship. And sure enough, at the end of all the making over of her, when she walked out of Miss Margaret's into the mall in a new pants-and-blouse outfit, wearing a pair of sandal shoes with ribbons on 'em—though she felt like her same ol' self, Henryetta knew she looked a sight—what with purple shadow on one eyelid and none on the other, finger and toe nails on the left side also purple, pink on the right, and her hair "tousled" and semi-dripping wet. "No! No! No!" Andy had said, before throwin' a glass of water on her and messin' up her hair-do. "She should look like she leads the active contemporary lifestyle of 'the younger Chelmsford Heights woman,' and just got off the yoga mat."

And Andy must've been right after all, 'cause none of the women she passed by looked at her like she hadn't been to the yogamat, or whatever.

Then Mr. Chester Grossman, at the door of his mall management office, looked right through her and said his waste basket didn't need to be emptied right then. When she reminded him of their interview appointment and re-explained that she worked for the *Weekender* and was writing up a history for the town's 50th anniversary, he let her in and was friendly enough. "Heck, I'm not <u>that</u> old," he said with a laugh, "call me Chester." But he still didn't pay her much notice after settin' down. He just went to staring at a telephone and tapping his fingers on his shiny desk, like he was real anxious for someone to call him. When she started spreading out some old photos, he barely glanced at the first row at all, but... "Hell, that's me," he said, grabbing one of the pictures out of a second row. "I'll be damned, just <u>look</u> at me!"

Henryetta got a pad and pencil out of her brand new "Louis Vuitton" satchel. "Were you comin' home from war or somethin'," she asked Mr. Chester, poised to write a caption for the picture of a young man in an army uniform. "Nah," he said, gazing at the sorta fuzzy image of his younger self. "I think this must be when I got kicked out of that crummy military school up in Missouri."

"Oh," she said.

"Oh, my god," he said, now looking at another photo. "What was her name, what <u>was</u> that gal's name? Oh yeah, June Marie, my first wife," he then said, and Henryetta jotted. "She doesn't live around here anymore," he then said, as if to explain his taking scissors from a drawer and cutting a young blonde woman out of a group picture. "Hand me that waste basket," he said, reaching for another archival photo, then another, and another, all including himself—almost all at parties, it seemed. And almost all in the company of various women—including several with a younger, thinner Phoebe Taliaferro-Dugan at his side—and then, several later pictorial records of "the good times with Evylene," his second wife, he said, as he ferociously "filed" clipped-off images of a tall, striking dark-haired woman into the waste basket. "Don't know exactly where in hell she is right now," he said, as blood from a finger he'd cut spilled onto her picture. "Wish I <u>could</u> get my hands on the…"

He looked at Henryetta with a kind of deranged smile. Pronouncing his ex-wife's name as "<u>Evil</u>ene," he said he was actually doing her a favor by "omitting" her from the town history 'cause she hated Chelmsford Heights and everything about it, "including the *Weekly Weekender*." Henryetta looked up from her note taking. "Evylene thought these…these party pics were part of a conspiracy to make her look bad, 'cause she's about half Indian and not a blonde," Mr. Chester said. "Even before our divorce, I was scared she might burn down the mall just to wipe out your office. She's spiteful that way."

Henryetta got to thinking that maybe this here Evylene could be the one who stole the *Weekender* archives and maybe murdered the man, Charlie Parker, who used to own the newspaper, but decided not to jump to any conclusion and compose it in her mind just yet. It could have been Mr. Chester who did it, she reckoned, as he went on acting crazy as a Betsy bug.

After about a half hour of so, an entire folder of photographs laid on the desk in two stacks: one of 'em severely edited by Mr. Chester and his scissors—all including a hairier-headed version of his own self—and the other one not. Henryetta didn't complain about his cutting, the *Weekender* had copies in storage, and she now had several pages of notes about both stacks of pictures, with names, occasions and approximate dates to go with 'em. "This is fun," Mr. Chester said, reaching for a second folder, and Henryetta couldn't help but wonder which he enjoyed most — looking at himself and remembering his younger days, or cropping out and forgetting all those women in his life, especially "Evilene." Anyway, if he kept on omitting he was gonna end up lookin' like he'd always been all alone.

Mr. Chester might just be goin' though one of those middle life crisises, Henryetta thought. He wasn't a naturally bad specimen, she reckoned — not like Leon Corn down in Henryetta. Bein' an heir an all, he was likely more like Dexter Durland, another ol' boy from her home town — rotten before he was ripe — 'cause his daddy owned the lumberyard and both Dairy Queens in town.

Out in the mall after the interview, Henryetta got back to thinking about Evylene Grossman. But even her ex-husband didn't seem to know where she could be found. And later...After getting back to the *Weekender* office and answering a telephone message waiting there for her — from Mrs. Mumu Taliaferro, her own self — she got another notion:

*Within twenty-four hours after seeing this investigative reporter taking notes about a Women's Alliance affair at her daughter's house, Mrs. Taliaferro, the Great Dame of the pack of ladies, called and suggested a meeting of just the two of them. The head of the Women's Alliance admitted she was "concerned" about this reporter's "lack of complete background information" related to what she might have seen and heard, and said she was "worried" about what this reporter might put in the upcoming special anniversary edition that the Alliance was paying for. This reporter had previously witnessed another local resident crop a batch of pictures that included his own self in the company of other women, maybe not wanting to be reminded of past marriages and romances, maybe not wanting his current wife to be reminded, or maybe not wanting her to find out about the other women for the first time. So...*

So for the meeting with Mrs. Taliaferro, Henryetta aimed to take along a pair of scissors with a big bunch of old photos. If Mrs. Mumu took the bait and went after the pictures like a goat in a patch of kudzu weeds, she might accidentally give away what it was that she and the Alliance wanted to hide, and why they stole the *Weekender* archives. It could be dangerous, handin' over a sharp tool to the someone who'd been "pleased" that the body of a Mr. Charlie Parker had been found right after the theft, and might have killed him her own self, but otherwise...

Otherwise, she was knee deep in difficulty, Henryetta admitted to herself. 'Cause she didn't have much of a story goin', and was gonna have to hustle like a one-armed fiddler to solve the mystery and put together a special edition of the paper by her deadline. Mr. Harold was counting on her, and she was determined to get the job done, whether she won one of those Pulitzer Prizes or not.

# TEN

Chester felt like he was watching barely soft-core pornography, as Bruno Camaleonte continued to seduce Shelley before his, her husband's very eyes. The pudgy, dark, curly-haired architect had greeted her at the door to his studio with a Russian-accented but Italian-sounding phrase that made her giggle, then had kissed her on both cheeks before thrusting a glass of red wine at her. Ignoring his real client, the man who paid his outrageous design fees, Camaleonte had then put an arm around Shelley's waist and shuffled her into his *"galleria de arte,"* where a chorus line of young lovelies made an aisle for them, and might as well have tossed rose pedals for their grand entrance. Faint, possibly mandolin music had begun to play in the background, as Camaleonte made a sweeping gesture with his free arm toward a brightly lit wall of colored architectural plans and sketches. "Off with the roof of this hideous mall!" he'd proclaimed, with a sidelong glance at Chester, the mall's owner in trust. "I want to see beautiful women in natural dappled light," he'd then said softly into Shelley's ear.

"And reigning over my new piazza—a thirty-foot fountain statue of Venus, her patina green with envy," he now said, nuzzling, "as you, *bella donna mia*, stroll past the lesser goddess to *Ceffo Friedrini's* fabulous footwear *bottega*, here where…" Chester pushed himself between them. "Keep your hands off her… that private space!" he blurted. "That's…that's Fanny O'Brien's boutique under a longterm lease. For now…I thought I made myself clear, Bruno, that you were to study only possibilities for only the other side of the Flying Flamingos Court." Maestro and bella donna looked into each other's eyes, seeming perhaps uncertain about which of them should ask him to leave. "Oh, for heaven's sake, Chester, you're such…such a study-fuddy," Shelley said, but Camaleonte cut her off with a wink. "Yes, of course, *il mio amico e mecenate*," said the sticky-tongued Russian, before giving his "friend and patron" a big Italian bear hug, then stepping back beside Shelley. "These concepts are for a grand master plan," he continued, "to be sculpted in stone-and-mortar when…as your personal circumstances"—he looked at Shelley—"dictate."

Taking her hand in his, Camaleonte moved to another illustration on the wall. "Here, on the 'other side' of the, uh, 'Fanny boutique,' Shelley will park her bicycle in a grove of imported fig trees, and in a Pleasant Peasant Earth Foods Market—here she will gather the all-natural essentials for her simple-but-elegant Tuscan lifestyle: her fresh, locally grown organic fruits and produce, her organic meats and poultry for sausage-making, her grains for hand-ground flours, her herbs, her spices, her garlics, her mustards, her…" Though Shelley's glossy lips puckered as Camaleonte continued laying out her groceries list, as though she were tasting her own homemade soup, or maybe about to kiss the chubby "supermarket delivery boy," Chester was dubious. He'd spent two-hundred fifty thousand dollars for "her" Tuscan-style kitchen—designed by Camaleonte—but except for dry cereal at breakfast and at catered dinner parties, he'd not had a meal at home since marrying Shelley. Recently, starved and intending to warm up a can of soup, he'd reached for a pan hanging from an antique rack, only to be scolded by his wife for moving the piece of copper cookware "decor." According to Shelley, she and all the other "professional women" of Chelmsford Heights — meaning mainly housewives with realtor licenses — desperately needed…

"…a gourmet cooking school over here," Camaleonte was saying, "next to her collectible wines cellar and…"

"How about a bank?" Chester suggested for the prominent outboard space. Having committed to pay for the 50th anniversary mall gala with funds the mall merchants association didn't have on hand — for which he'd almost, but not quite gotten laid — he was desperate to establish a fresh banking relationship, and by offering a prime branch location to… "Really, Chester," Shelley said, rolling her big blue eyes, "all you ever think about is money and…Brunie has barely enough room for a day spa, as it is."

"For her work outs, her interpretive dance, her yoga, her pilates," added "her" architect, though under *Day Spa* on the proposed floor plan, the word *Salon* was listed most prominently, with *Foot Facials* among its sub-categories of *Activities of a Healthy Contemporary Lifestyle*. Chester felt more depressed, but then Shelley moved away from "Brunie" and put a diamond encrusted hand on the outlined box labelled *Pleasant Peasant Earth Foods Market*. And her lips now looked more pursed than puckered — a sure sign that she too was dubious of the market's concept and was about to change her mind. "I love your mind, Brunie," she said, "and your shoes, but 'earthy' is just not 'me' anymore, and Tuscany — it's so yesterday." Chester's heart skipped a beat. Finally, the sensible woman he'd fallen for seven years ago had returned to…

"There's a new, cutting edge chain of upscale supermarkets in California," she said. "They're French and so...so...so 'lifestyle.' All the food is already cooked, which is soooo today! Their orchids are to..."

"*Magnifique! mon chérie!*" said Bruno Camaleonte, leaping the Alps from Italy to France in a single bound. "Cutting edge," Shelley had said, those were among the favorite buzz words of a female real estate broker who for many years had handled the leasing of space in Chelmsford Heights Mall. To Chester they had the whine of a buzz saw, slashing cash flow to the bone. Through the years there had been numerous such "soooo today" stores come along, and inevitably...The Sharper Image came to Chester's mind as having been, years ago, the quintessential cutting edge trendy retail chain that the broker, Didi Finegan... She didn't know stone from stone-washed cotton, mortar from mohair,but had talked Leo into effectively <u>paying</u> the electronic gadgets catalogue merchant to occupy fully fixtured space at a total landlord cost the mall had nowhere near recovered by the time the merchandising gimmick got dull as a twice-told tale, and the the chain went out of business. And since then, Chester himself had fallen for Didi's...

"And Brunie," Shelley was now saying, "Pepe's Yogawear—it's made entirely of seaweed from Martinique and is one hundred percent biodegradable, which is soo..."

"Martinique? *Magnifique!*"

Chester dismissed a notion that Shelley would involve herself in anything more than innocent flirting with Camaleonte. It had taken her years—and respectable marriage to him—for her to claw her way back into Chelmsford Heights society. She would never again risk the danger of bad publicity by getting caught in anything illicit, he thought, turning away as she and her architectural designer continued jabbering in bad French. Aimlessly, he wandered to another wall, this one plastered with black-and-white materials, including, he couldn't help but notice, several framed pages from a years-old trade magazine called *Lifestyle Shopping Centers Today*. They were copies of an article titled *DE-CONSTRUCTION OF THE AMERICAN SHOPPING MALL, New Cutting Edge Concepts for Upscale Suburban Lifestyle*, by who else but Bruno Camaleonte, *AIA, AAA, AA*. Chester skimmed the maestro's bullet points:

- *ANCHORS AWAY - Heave-ho the dead weight of old fashioned department stores owned by barnacled captains of ancient capitalism. Set shopping malls a sail...*
- *RAZE THE ROOF - Rip out their dirty ducts! Neither snow nor rain nor sleet nor heat, nor gloomy day or night will keep the upscale American shopper from her appointed task. Down with Heating! Down with Ventilation! Down with Air Conditioning! Down with...*
- *WAKE UP AMERICA - Smell the coffee here, the fresh baked breads there, NOT in an antiseptic food court! All the odors of a movable feast — the pizza, the bar b-q, the fried chicken livers, the burgers, the fries, the apple pies — and the glorious bouquet of onions EVERYWHERE ! It's the new aromatherapy for...*
- *POWER TO THE PEOPLE - Developers and shoppers of suburbia, UNITE! You have nothing to lose but your boring cookie-cutter chain stores. Bring back our moms and pops from Floridian exile. Man the barricades for...*
- *UNFOCUS GROUPTHINK - Ask not what the demographically elite need or want. Sell them what you desire them to desire. Brainwashing studies show...*

Chester had never realized how radical the open-air specialty shopping center movement had become, how big a threat so-called lifestyle centers posed to malls. Bruno Camaleonte, an obvious foreigner from the East Coast, if not off-shore somewhere, might be a communist, he thought, or an anarchist, out to destroy…On a large aerial photograph mounted on the wall, a target had been drawn in red, with its bull's eye superimposed directly on top of Chelmsford Heights Mall, and…Chester's attention was distracted by something else he saw in the birds eye view of the local area. Something was going on in Evylene's Fiddler's Green Cemetery across Trolley Street. He waved to one of Camaleonte's young assistants. "What's this here?" he asked, after the young lovely had come to his side. He put a finger on the aerial photo. She leaned forward, squinting. "It looks like some kind of…maybe a portable derrick for some kind of drilling," she said, "or maybe a large wench or small crane for…"

"Drilling? Drilling for what?" Chester asked. "Oil? Is she… Damnit! Are they fracking down there?"

"Maybe, but I doubt it," the young female architect or engineer said. "The ground is already unstable and…See over here, since they excavated for that new six-lane road at the south end, the whole terrain is shifting. It's almost dangerous. I heard they'd closed off access, and…See, this shot was taken only last week—they're putting up a new fence, electrified, someone said."

"Electrified?! Sumbitch! And what about this?" Chester asked, putting a finger directly across Trolley Street from a mall parking lot at the Macy's end. "Oh, that's for a new storm sewer," the woman answered. "They're tunneling under Trolley Street and…"

"Yes, Chester, *mi ami*," said Camaleonte, suddenly on his other side, licking his lips like some kind of European lizard. "I know what you're zinking, *mi patron*, and it is sad, very *tres triste*."

"What?! What am I zinking? And how would you know anything about it?" Chester asked, though certain the wife of his accomplice, "Mrs. X," had blabbed about the planned mission to rescue his mother's remains from Fiddler's Green Cemetery.

"Everybody knows," the sumbitch answered. "And it's so obvious to…an educated eye. You threw away a pearl far more valuable zan Chelmsford Heights Mall. Zee cemetery site would have been *sans imperfection* for a major lifestyle shopping center. Shelley, she is so, so…*decu*…for you."

# ELEVEN

Gates at all entrances to Chelmsford Heights had for years been a pet project of Mayoress Taliaferro's. So when Her Honoress announced that the gates construction contract would not be opened for bidding, Chief Bulldog thought she understood why she'd been summoned to a private meeting in the mayoral office in ye olde town hall—also attended by an unidentified, thin, dark-haired man. To reinforce the major Welcome-and-Warning signs at its main entrance, the town had recently completed construction of marble-clad pillars on both sides of all streets leading into the Heights—those to the left adorned with ornate plaques etched with the word "Welcome," those to the right with matching hand-carved pieces inscribed "Residents Only." But now—without iron gates mounted on the columns, except for decoration, what was the point of the second, if not the first message? "Your Honoress," Bulldog said, rising from her chair, "if I may...?"

"You may not," said Mrs. Taliaferro. "This is not about security, Chief O'Connor, it's about...budgetary consideration," she said, after glancing at the thin man. Bulldog lowered her Big Behind to its prior resting place in a hard wood chair. Later this evening she would run some numbers to show that longterm costs of increased police manpower versus the one-time tab for the gates would... "And Chief," said the mayoress, "due to those same, uh, considerations, I'm afraid you're going to have to downsize." Chief O'Connor, shocked, started to sweat. Downsize? Who was the thin, dark-haired man at the table? Probably an auditor, she thought, a small minded bean counter from the private sector who didn't know beans from boysenberries about the "budgetary considerations" of law enforcement. "Well," said Bulldog, "one or two of my officers are nearing early retirement age. I suppose... maybe I could..."

"By at least fifty percent," the mayoress continued. "You need to get down to half your size by the end of the month, and make a personal commitment..." Bulldog instinctively sucked in her ample gut, though Mrs. Taliaferro herself... "to either a police car or motorcycle year-round, not both. As for your salary..." Maybe in reaction to her subordinate's obvious distress—sweat poured from every Bulldog pore—the mayoress paused, then added, "we're all making lifestyle sacrifices. Indeed, as a D.A.R.V.I.P., it pains me to say..." She paused again, took a deep breath, and in a manner that sounded to Bulldog too poor to paint, too proud to white wash, the mayoress explained that "so as to not overlap, and detract from our town's fiftieth anniversary observances, I have decided to cancel the 4th of July!

"It's all Chester Grossman's fault!" she then practically shouted at the thin man. "Mall sales are down, sales tax revenues are down—we may even have to assess real estate taxes on our homes! And on top of all this, Chester..." At the sight of a not so subtle throat-cutting gesture by the now swarthy-looking, dark-eyed thin man, Mrs. Taliaferro fell silent. Bulldog, despite herself, squirmed in her uncomfortable chair, wedging her sweat-soaked boxers deeper between her steaming buns. "May I call you Rosie?" the man asked, leaning across the table toward her, "or would you prefer—is it Miss or Missus O'Connor?" he queried, with a yellow-toothed smile, looking hungry as a mangy wolf. "I understand, Rosie, that you have…a 'close' relationship with Chester Grossman," he continued, making "close" sound like "cozy," at least. "Nothing wrong with that as a 'personal'…Your personal 'affairs' are your own business, but…Has Mr. Grossman, or any of his mall employees or tenants, ever given you anything of value for your, uh, personal 'services'?"

Not for half an hour after their "friendly chat," while taking a hot, sudsy shower in the police department locker room, did Bulldog fully understand: she was the game afoot. The thin man, who had never really come clean about who he was and what he was up to, had the sweaty smell of a lawyer about him, Chief Bulldog now realized—no doubt hired by the town to help it weasel out of responsibility for her allegedly wrongful arrest of a suspected mall shoplifter. They were coming after her to get at Chester Grossman, trying to make it look like she was on the take, protecting Grossman's mall racket, and not the innocent women and children of Chelmsford Heights, when she chased after the speeding black Honda through a red light at Trolley Street and…

Bulldog re-lathered between her legs and tried not to worry. Her relationship with Mr. Grossman had always been strictly professional, not "personal," cordial but not "close." All her dealings with him, his mall employees and tenants, had always been aboveboard, nothing had ever passed under the table or on it…except for a few food court freebies from time to time as she worked the Rodeo Drive beat—slices of pizza…chicken wings…dozens of egg rolls…hamburgers…hot dogs…cheese fries...buns...tacos...fishsticks...pretzels...kebobs...bagels... soft drinks...coffee...an apple...and recently... She re-lathered again.

Later, feeling clean as a baby's bottom—Bulldog had never tended to infants—the chief got herself dressed in civvies and walked across the so-called "Mason-Dixon Line" to the dirty side of Trolley Street. At the counter of the Chew-n-Choke truck stop cafe...She hardly recognized that new reporter for the *Weekly Weekender*, Henryetta Something-or-Other, who was sitting on a stool, all prettied up in a dress, waiting for her. The little runt was persistent as a cat scratching at a tile floor after doing its business. And when she'd caught...when she'd <u>followed</u> a law enforcement officer on covert patrol to the garbage room of truck dock number four, and seen the officer seizing a pink Peek-a-Boo panty girdle as evidence of...possibly body snatching or possibly some other illegal activity, well, Bulldog had tentatively dismissed her suspicions of the girl's involvement in those crimes and agreed to meet with her. She'd said she was putting together a special edition of the *Weekender*, made-up of newspaper stories from prior years, for Chelmsford Heights' fiftieth anniversary, and wanted to add some personal "color" to the previously published *Police Blotter* features. Bulldog saw no harm in making a personal contribution to a write-up of town history, as long as the coloration didn't apply to matters Mrs. Taliaferro had personally bleached out.

"I sure am obliged to you for takin' the time to meet with me, Ms. Bulldog," the girl said, after the chief had sat down and waved to a waitress for a cup of forty-weight and mud balls for two. "Like I said before, I'm new in town and—no offense to you intended—for the life of me, I can't see what could be so interesting to folks around here about the paper's 'Police Blotter' reportin'." Bulldog was not offended, but she was puzzled. "How far back have you gone?" she asked. Prior to Mrs. Taliaferro taking over ye olde town hall about four years ago, the *Blotter* had told some pretty danged exciting tales of local law breaking and law enforcement, with plenty of color to 'em. "Before my time," the chief said, "but that spree of semi-sexual assaults one summer must have made interesting reading to some." The Henryetta girl looked at her like she'd never heard, or read about the infamous "Masked Pollinator"—rumored have turned out to be a prominent Chelmsford Heights resident, Bulldog had heard—who disguised himself as a bumble bee, stalked young daisies and lilies in private gardens, and was finally apprehended by Bulldog's predecessor only after forcing himself on every Black-eyed Susan in Lord Chelmsford Park. "And, I don't wanna sound like I'm braggin'," Bulldog said, "but I was up in that tree in the mall food court for three days and nights coaxing that boy's suicidal parakeet off its perch. It was all in your paper's *Police Blotter*, 'cept the colorful part about me gettin' a medal."

The little strawberry blonde reporter looked up from scribbling in a notebook. "Do you recall what that boy's name was?" she asked. "And the parakeet's? 'Cause correct journalism requires..." Bulldog got a whiff of something tainted—and it wasn't the Chew-n-Choke blue plate special this time. "Then of course there was that would-be burglar I shot dead in Mrs. Taliaferro's front yard on Christmas Eve," she said, giving the *Weekender* writer a sideways eye ball. "He was an old man with white whiskers, carrying a Salvation Army kettle and a big red sack of..." The newspaper girl looked up from her notebook again, eyes big and round. "You did <u>what</u>?!" she said, looking shocked—but just for a second, before getting back to her jotting. "What was <u>his</u> name?" she asked. "And what was in the sack? Are you sure...?"

Hah! Just as Bulldog had detected: the little cub reporter hadn't done her homework. She hadn't thoroughly read the back issues of the *Weekly Weekender Police Blotter* or even the front pages of past *Weekenders*, and that had to be…Misleading a police officer had to be strongly discouraged, dog-gone-it!

Bulldog didn't have to find and use a rubber hose on the suspect—just a body slam to the cafe's linoleum tile floor and a set of cuffs—to make her begin to see the error of her criminal ways. Oh yeah, the perp came clean soon enough, but like most petty criminals, tried to blame her scam on a "big boss" she referred to as a "Mr. Harold," who… "don't want the police to know nothin'," she now wailed, "so I can't tell…" Bulldog applied more pressure with her knee. "How many filthy Marlboros have you smoked in truck dock number four? Whose body have you snatched today?" she demanded to be told. "Dang it!" the prisoner yelped, "the back issues of the *Weekender* with the old *Police Blotter* features in 'em are missing. Someone stole 'em, prob'ly 'cause they don't want the truth about somethin' to come out in *The New York Times* or the *USA Today*, dang it!"

Bulldog eased off a little. Somebody stole the old *Weekender Police Blotters*? Yeah, there was something else afoot, she thought, and…Unable to detect the stench of Marlboro smoking on the suspect's breath, and by nature afflicted with a forgiving heart, Bulldog removed the cuffs, let the little newspaper girl get up from the floor and—by the book—said to a circle of onlookers: "Nothin' goin' on here, folks. Go on back to your supper." She then turned back to…her name possibly was Henryetta. "Okay," she said, dusting the girl off some, "that's two balls against you, Missy. One…two more, and you're…you <u>walk</u>!"

Outside, strolling in the night air, trying to relax but still worried about a gateless Chelmsford Heights, illegal cigarette smoking in truck dock number four and suspicions of a body snatching ring led by Chester Grossman's ex-wife, Bulldog was surprised to see Pop Barnett on duty in front of the rusting, formerly pearly white gates at the cemetery corner, sitting in the disabled Fiddler's Green police car—now wheeless as well as tireless, and up on blocks. She slid into the front seat next to her fellow crime fighter. "Thought you always worked the graveyard shift, Pop," she said, after first asking the old cop how his hammer was hangin' and being told, as usual, that it was bent for Lent. "Used to like the graveyard hours—better class of truckers on the road after midnight," he said, holding up his CB microphone, "but..." He nodded toward the cemetery grounds. "There's somethin' mighty strange goin' on in there, Bulldog," he said. "It could be the Masons, putting up dead bodies in their jars, like some people say, but I'm pretty sure it's my late ex-wife, Irene, turned into a demon succubus and..."

"Succubus?!"

"Waitin' for me to fall asleep, so she can have her way with me. That's why they put up that electrified fence—to keep her where she belongs, but..." Bulldog had never heard of a demon succubus in this part of the state, or anywhere else. She'd been told the electrified fence was to keep varmints, vandals, picnickers and trysters out of the Fiddler's Green graveyard while it was being re-stocked. "And she's cut me off from all my CB good buddies," Pop said, again holding up his CB microphone. "Caught me...hell, it was only innocent flirtin' 'tween me and Little Bo Peep from Omaha, but zap! That was Irene's doin' alright. She was always insanely jealous 'cause of my good looks, and insanely ever'thing else too. Now all I can tune in is Irene her own self, singin' lullaby love songs to me," he said, turning a knob of his old CB radio. "Listen, Bulldog, but just for a few seconds or you'll wake up in the morning with your pants took off, like me last Sunday."

Bulldog heard only a burst of static, but... "Look!" Pop said, after jerking his head around toward the cemetery. "She's out there now, sparkin' with ever' danged man in uniform who comes along, the no account hussy!" Bulldog looked toward the cemetery. In the foreground, she did see sparks, caused by electrocution of bugs and insects flying into the electrified fence, but...Yes, in the darkened distance inside the burial ground, she saw larger, longer lasting flickers of light and...She almost jumped out of her boxers at the sound of Irene singing...*take off your shoosies, dear/and loosen up your tie*...or maybe it was Bette Midler. Not in the mood to find out the hard way, Bulldog jumped out of the Fiddler's Green police car and hustled back toward the Chew-n-Choke, with Pop Barnett hurrying after her.

# TWELVE

Willis Willis jotted *Evylene Grossman* on a client billing form, together with date and time of day, and began dictating letters into a recorder: "Dear Mrs. Green, re: your letter of the 24th. In order for my client, Fiddler's Green Cemetery, Inc., to undertake disinterment of Aunt Wanda per your request, it is necessary for you to to fill-out, sign by notarized signature and return the enclosed form, together with an initial, non-refundable deposit in the amount of Five Thousand Dollars ($5,000). Etcetera. Same letters to Mr. and Mrs. Brown re: disinterment of her parents — deposit of Ten Thousand required — and to Mr. Golden with regard to digging up his late wife, uh, Ethel."

He went on to the next stack of letters: "Dear Mrs. Black, re: status of grave removal. On behalf of my client, Fiddler's Green Cemetery, Inc., I am pleased to inform you that remains believed to be those of Grandpa Willie have been disinterred from the cemetery as requested and authorized by you, and are now stored in a reasonably cool facility. As you were previously apprised was a possibility, however, as per numerous conditions and regulations found to be applicable in this case, said remains cannot be released to you unless and until DNA analysis confirms your kinship with them. This will require an additional non-refundable deposit in the amount of Five Thousand Dollars ($5,000), payable within ten days of this notice. Please refer to enclosed forms and plastic bag of Q-tips for swabbing. Etcetera. Same letter, with appropriate remains names to the Smiths, the Joneses, the Rices, Leonards and Mosses.

"Dear Mrs. Parker, re: your recent inquiry, the answer is yes. Based on existence of a steel plate found in the skull of remains recently unearthed from Fiddler's Green Cemetery, we can confirm that said remains are indeed those of your late husband. The plate is inscribed with a signature and sentiment of his former secretary, however, and given the size and weight of the dang thing—along with the intimate nature of the inscription—perhaps the memento should go to her and the remains to you for cremation and inurnment in the Chelmsford Heights Hall of Fame. Etcetera. Bill both the wife and the girlfriend too, if she's still alive after all these years.

"Dear Mrs. Williams nee: Coates, re: terms of grave removal. In reply to your letter of the 25th, please be again advised, regrettably, that the remains of your late husband, Jay J. Coates, are no longer welcome at Fiddler's Green Cemetery, nor are refunds of your non-refundable payments possible. In answer to your question, yes, the hole has already been filled in. Unless we are informed otherwise within ten days, Jay J.'s remains will be sent to you, at your added cost and expense, in Hawaii. P.S. I am sorry that this complicates your honeymoon, and I wish you the best in your new marriage. If things don't work out, give me a call.

"Dear Mrs. Horton, re: visitation rights. In reply to your letter of the 25th, unless and until my client, Fiddler's Green Cemetery, Inc., receives your non-refundable deposit—for the very reason that the remains believed to be those of your late runaway husband, R.E., could be, as you yourself say, 'a case of mistaken identity'—unless and until DNA testing is paid for and completed, we must deny your request to 'look the remains in the eye.' Furthermore, please be advised that even after your taking possession of what's left of R.E., it would be against the law for you to 'fetch a skillet up against' his…"

At the creaking sound of his office door opening, Willis looked up from his dictation. "Someone here to see you, Willis," said his assistant, Clara, with a faint smile. "A woman—says it's about something 'personal' and 'tray' confidential," she added, with the smile changed to a smirk. "Better get into your 'country lawyer' character for Mrs. Chester Grossman, her own ever lovin' self." Willis jumped to his feet, loosened his stained tie, undid a button on his semi-clean shirt and searched his desktop for a straw or toothpick to chew on. He'd talked to Evylene by phone only day before yesterday. She was in the U.S. but had said nothing about coming to… "It's the semi-new one," Clara said, this time with a sneer.

A blonde woman, about forty, beautiful in a made-up sort of way but thin as thirsty cattle, walked…No, Shelley Grossman pranced into Willis' office, as though modeling her finery on the runway of a fashion show. "Just water," she said, after sitting down on the other side of Willis' desk, "*Evian* in a wine glass, no ice, and…" Clara slammed the door shut and Willis sat down. "I want a divorce, from Chester Grossman, for an off-price legal fee, not a penny more," Shelley Grossman said. "I won't haggle about alimony, I just want the mall and…Our *chateau* on Viceroy Lane—or as I prefer, *LeRoi Soleil*—is worth at least two million, the lake house about half that. And the life insurance…" Willis raised a hand try to slow her down, but she went on "shopping," so to speak, 'til dropping—after listing, "his Rolex knock-off that I charged to him for three thousand, a German coffee maker in his office that's worth a few bucks, and his shoes—Chester buys handmade shoes from London, sub-size 10, at twenty-five hundred a pop.

"Also Versus—I'm told your opponents call you 'Versus'," she then said. "I want you to prove beyond a shadow of doubt that I am completely innocent of the murder of Tutu Taliaferro-Dugan. I would never have paid..."

"Murder?! Mrs. Grossman, I'm just a country lawyer, trying to...Are you armed? Have you called the police? Clara..."

"No, because at least one cop is in on it. And the murder is not 'going down'—how appropriate for Tutu—until Mr. X gets back from a karaoke tournament in Branson, Missouri. I was only...only venting when I told Chester he had to...do it for me."

After a lot of confused back-and-forth between them, Willis had a renewed keen understanding of why he himself had never gotten married, and a loose grasp of the loose parts rattling around in Shelley Grossman's pretty little head. In a nutshell, she'd overheard snippets of a telephone conversation between her husband and a man known to her by voice as a Chelmsford Heights policeman who regularly responded to her emergency calls. After her husband, Chester, told his co-conspirator something about "new information on how to sneak up on her," they had discussed financial terms of hiring two thugs, a Mr. X and a Mr. O, to "get her at all costs." That was just like Chester, she said, "not a nickel's worth of common sense about money." She'd also heard the cop say something to the effect that "she" was as good as dead or would be dead for a long time, and then her husband whimpering that "she was the only other woman who ever sort of loved me."

The intended victim is obviously Tutu," she then said, in response to Willis' skepticism. "They—Chester and Tutu—have been fighting about me and my major part in the fiftieth anniversary show. Tutu's soooo jealous of me and my much younger, so 'today' lifestyle—and I'd said to Chesty, just days before, that if he expected me to ever again, you know, 'do it,' he was going to have to… I might have said get rid of Tutu, referring only to her as Co-Chairlady of the Anniversary Celebration Committee, not as the 'other' woman. The two of them started, you know, 'doing it' in college, and I suspect have carried on and off since then, if you can believe it. Poor dear, she's lost a ton, but do you remember how she looked a few years ago when she had her pictures <u>spread</u> all over the *Weekender* <u>every</u> week? 'Shown here, Mrs. Phoebe Taliaferro-Dugan, filling the club ballroom like she was wearing it, with Mr. Chester Grossman peeking out from…' I don't really care if they're, you know, 'doing it', but Tutu <u>and</u> her awful mother…"

"What makes you so sure your husband wasn't talking to his accomplice about <u>you</u>, your own self, as the intended victim?" Willis said. "I'm just a country lawyer, but…"

"Me?!" she exclaimed, her big blue eyes up to the rims in bewilderment. "Why on earth would Chester…"

"Well, like I say, I'm just a country lawyer," said Willis, "but I have noticed a thing or two through the years about divorce situations, and I happen to know your husband has been carrying a heavy burden of…"

"Oh, pooh, enough about Tutu, she's a big, a *tres* big girl," said Shelley Grossman. "Let's get back to the business of the mall."

"Now hold on there, Mrs. Grossman," Willis said, buttoning his shirt, struggling to get out of character. "I ain't your country lawyer—I cain't be. I've got conflicts of interest and...I cain't get into it all, but from what I hear, Chester's mall bidness ain't so good right now. He only 'owns' the mall property 'in trust,' and there's probably not much current value to it after takin' into account its condition and the debt on it. Same for the houses you mentioned. So you might wanna start thinkin' 'bout settlin'..."

"For life insurance? A fake Rolex? Some old worn out shoes and a coffee pot? After all the times I've let him, you know, 'do it,' is that what you're...?"

Well, not exactly, I'm just sayin' that you might wanna think about patchin' up things with Chester. Maybe give him some, you know, 'sugar', if that's what it takes to calm him down some before he goes and gets somebody killed."

"Well!" she said, up on her high heels, "my friends were certainly wrong about yew, Mr. Willis 'Versus' Willis. You're not such a good blood sucking ball buster after all. Evylene got the cemetery and has made a fortune from...There's money...and lifestyle to be made from that so yesterday mall, and I'm not about to lay down again to get what I've already put out plenty enough for!"

After Shelley Grossman stormed out of his office, Willis leaned back in his chair and made a "steeple" with the fingers of both hands. Immediately upon hearing of her desire for a divorce, he'd begun to worry that the current Mrs. Grossman would fall into the grasp of "a good ball busting blood sucker"—such as Morty Wolfe, for instance, a local lawyer, thin as a fiddle string himself, and hungry as she was. Wolfe had been hired by the town of Chelmsford Heights to defend against Willis' lawsuit about its police chief's wrongful arrest of an old woman for shoplifting, so he too might have a conflict of interest if Shelley Grossman went to him, but…If Chester had broken under the pressures bearing on him, and had talked about hiring "hit men," his intended victim would likely be, Willis reckoned—not his old girlfriend, Tutu, nor his current estranged wife, Shelley, but…Willis worried that it was much more likely that Chester Grossman was out to "get at all costs" his ex-wife, Evylene, even though he seemed to think she was the only "other" woman who "ever sort of loved him." And Evylene Grossman, dad-gum-it, was Willis' best client!

# THIRTEEN

Henryetta thought she must be the only unpatriotic American who ever lived, for not bein' too disappointed that Chelmsford Heights had to cancel the 4th of July. She would have had to cover the scheduled parade, the ceremonies, the speeches and the fireworks for next Friday's *Weekender*, which would have left her even further behind in puttin' together the special anniversary edition for publication in just ten more days and nights. She had lots and lots of material, but also gaps, she'd realized, after spreadin' out her stuff on the living room floor of her rent house this morning and going over it all day. Gettin' confused as a goat on shag carpet, she'd decided not to go by the years, and instead organize the piece around *Weekender* regular features, with emphasis on the more recent times. Some of the older ones were deadly dull to her, but…Mrs. Hardcroft, for instance, even after givin' such a wordy interview about her family trees and the town's new "Call-'n-bury-'em" place for ancestor ashes, had sent in a letter about one old feature that Henryetta reckoned she was gonna have to take into account: *My Dear Miss Hebert…* etcetera…etcetera…

*...and as I may have neglected to mention during our recent chat, many of us have been sorely disappointed in Weekender reportage of community affairs since Mr. Mixon came to town from God only knows what backwater. As stated by Mrs. Taliaferro in a letter-to-the editor that he neglected to publish, he has, in particular, displayed gross insensitivity to matters related to our ancestry, as exemplified by a front page article last month headlined HORSES' ASHES HONORED AT CEREMONY. But again, I digress.*

*My main purpose in writing is to re-emphasize how much we treasured the Weekender's regular "Where Are They Now" features published by the newspaper's former owner. Yes, definitely, in answer to your request for guidance, those old photographs of the headstones at the resting places of our dearly departed should be the very centerpiece of the upcoming 50th anniversary edition. And while I recognize the difficulties, even the dangers of reporting on matters related to distressful conditions currently afflicting Fiddler's Green Cemetery, how wonderful it would be to see that some of those headstones still proudly stand, that some of those remains of our forefathers are still safely at rest, awaiting disinterment from that foreign ground and glorious return to Chelmsford Heights for inurnment in our Hall of Fame. I could go on and on about...*etcetera...

*In closing, I would like to remind you that the correct spelling of...* etcetera...

*Yours very truly...*

*P.S. etcetera.*

Feeling a little tired, Henryetta put the letter aside. But then, in the shower, she kept on thinking about it. She would have liked to look into the real news story about strange cemetery goin's on that Mr. Harold had told her about, but she didn't have the time. If anything, she needed a break, and for tonight was lookin' forward to just watching an old picture show on TV about a gal news reporter—*Woman of the Year*—and forgettin' about such unimportant things as old pictures of headstones and conspiracy theories about grave robberies. But just as she got out of the shower with a wet head o' hair, someone came bangin' on the front door.

Standin' on the porch, a boy about her age—with pale white skin, dark blue eyes, and a shock of straight black hair hangin' down across half his forehead… "Hi, I'm from across the street," he said, "and…" Henryetta glanced past him, saw the black hearse was back, and…her heart pert near jumped out at him. "My friend from out of town needs a cab to the airport," he said. "For some reason, she would prefer not to ride in the back of my…" They laughed together when it hit 'em both at once: <u>his</u> hearse…her yellow Checker…proving that you can't tell nothin' about a body inside a house from what kind of vehicle you see parked in the driveway.

And silly her, she thought later, she shouldn't have put her jeans and tee-shirts in the washin' machine. She should have known the boy from across the street, Billy O'Dell, would come back over after droppin' off his friend—an older looking, tall, dark-haired woman she'd seen standing by the hearse. Now all she had to put on was a pretty dress. Stepping out onto the front porch with Billy, she heard music in the distance. Later on, maybe, there would be fireworks, she reckoned.

They walked on up to Persimmon Street—and into a cloud of marijuana smoke thicker than the drug store perfume at her high school prom. A big party was goin' on in the middle of a block, and though most of the people looked like they were probably under forty, they were sorta costumed as old hippies. It was the "Boho" look from "Portlandia" that Amanda had tried to get her into at Miss Margaret's store. Lots of guys had pony tails, lots of the girls wore mood rings, all of which made Henryetta feel like she was standin' out a little too much in her pink feed-sack print dress and kinda dressy sandal shoes. That might have been part of why the Bohos didn't seem particularly friendly toward her and Billy, she thought. And as the two of 'em walked around in the crowd, she started gettin' a feeling that Fiddlers—as people living in Fiddler's Green were called—weren't so much different from the folks in Chelmsford Heights in thinkin' they were about the best and brightest thing to come along since bare feet, and apparently, that outside "others" were out to get them. Mercy, she'd never heard such serious well informed conversation at a keg party.

"They have a secret plan," she overheard one of the Fiddler's say, "they're just waiting for the right moment to spring it on us. That's why I keep my stash buried in a backyard flower bed, and always keep a baseball bat under my pillow. It's the big oil companies, they want another war."

"Yeah, I'm gonna get a Tibetan K-9 for protection," said another Fiddler. "They… I'd rather not be too specific, but it's the C.I.A. alright. They're digging a secret tunnel under Trolley Street, so the next thing will be for 'em to pave over the cemetery for a landing strip. I play a lot of video war games, so I know…"

"They'll sneak under the Mason-Dixon Line an' pave our town cemetery over my dead body," said another one. "It's the only green space we have left, and this side of Planet Earth south of Trolley Street belongs to the people, or ought to. We should get up a petition against whatever it is they're up to."

"No, it's not gonna be an air strip, from what I hear. It's Wall Street sons of bitches and they're gonna put in a country club just for women and purebred dogs, with a golf course. It'll stay green, but private unless we get organized and do something about it. Hey, let's get that petition goin'."

"There'll be a private country club for those rich Mason bitches over my dead body. The chemicals they use to keep a golf course green would kill all the wildlife around here. The property rightfully belongs to Mother Nature's own…"

"Yeah, that's what I read somewhere. Donald Trump's in charge and they're gonna develop the cemetery into a private wildlife preserve, so those rich bitches can shoot birdies and…"

"Over my dead body. This town is short of fowl life as it is."

They ought to just pave the sumbitch over and put in a high-priced shopping center for those rich bitches, with a bridge over Trolley Street to connect with Macy's. Let's put that in the petition. Then maybe we could get ourselves a fire truck and some new wheels for our police car."

"My cousin works for a guy who actually <u>knows</u> Pop Barnett—he's the freakin' <u>Chief</u> of Police and is wise to <u>everything</u> goin' on around here. He has actually <u>seen</u> aliens out there in the cemetery at night, looking for signs of intelligent life and doing things to dead bodies that would curl…"

"Over my dead body…"

"Illegal Mexicans in the cemetery at night, yeah, that fits with what I've heard. They ain't just mowin' grass, amigo."

Henryetta noticed Billy kinda chuckle about all the local jabberin', so she reckoned none of it amounted to much. Billy was, after all, from a long line of undertakers, he'd told her when they were walking over to the party. So he likely knew all about cemetery goin's on, and because of the heat, he himself worked nights. She cottoned quite a bit to Billy O'Dell. He was a real gentleman, she thought, as he went off to find another cup of beer for her. There was just somethin' about him that… "Oh my gawd! it's <u>yew</u> again," said Kuku Taliaferro, of all people. "No way, can't be," Chef Gregory then said, sidling up to her. "They must have put you through a car wash and…" And danged if Henryetta didn't feel the sumbitch rubbin' her fanny.

She wheeled around on him and grabbed his crotch. "Where I come from, which happens to be down the road in Henryetta, a gentleman don't go feelin' up other gals right in front of this own date," she said, squeezing. He yelped somethin' fierce. "Oh my gawd, please don't put this in the paper," Kuku wailed. "My mother…" She turned to flee and…Dad-gum-it ! Kuku was wearin' <u>her</u> jeans, the ones with the John Deere patch on the butt that she'd traded in at Miss Margaret's store in the mall, and…Kuku turned back around, looking like she'd been caught shopliftin', or somethin'. "My grandmother would kill me if she knew about…" She looked toward Chef Gregory. "Don't wet my used Levis, Kuku," Henryetta said, lettin' go of her hold on the stuck-up Tri Phi Phi gal's secret boyfriend. "I just wanted to know how and what <u>yew</u> feel when you got your own hand up under Greggie's apron. I got a picture of you doin' that, but now that I know it ain't no big news, I probably <u>won't</u> put in the paper."

"I would," said someone from behind her. Henryetta turned around. "I'm Clara," said a dark-haired gal with a sorta noticeable mustache, holding out a hand to shake. She had a firm grip, and kinda had the look of a youngish "old maid" who'd been sharpening her own hatchet for lack of a man to do it for her. "*The Guillotine* will publish your photo and your jibe," she said, "with a header: 'Little Miss Chelmsford Heights Plays With Kitchen Help's Dick'. A <u>real</u> journalist…If you <u>were</u> one, you would show and tell what you felt, not give a damn about how <u>she</u> felt."

Henryetta noticed Billy—holdin' two cups of beer—hangin' back while she talked to Clara, a professional colleague from a local newspaper she'd not heard of. And awhile later, he seemed real curious about what they'd been talking about, but… The Fiddlers were gettin' restless and some a little rowdy. "Damn them damn Masons on the other side. What are they up to now?" said one of 'em, settin' in a lawn chair, with two cups of beer in hand for hisself. "They know some of us work for a living and gotta get up early, that's why they're waitin' so late to shoot off the fireworks, I bet," he said. "I'm about ready to start raisin' some hell about it!"

So Henryetta took Billy's hand in hers and suggested, well, what she had in mind was maybe them settin' on the divan in her rent house and maybe lightin' each other's fuses, so to speak. But on the way back to her place, she got a feeling she'd about ruined the mood by paying so much attention to Clara, and when they got back and she opened the front door to…Dang it, she'd forgot her living room, including the divan, was covered with *Weekender* work. For lettin' her career ambition get in the way—just like Katherine Hepburn in *Woman of the Year*—all the sparkin' she got was a little ol' kiss under the porch light.

And even later, layin' in bed by herself, her mind wouldn't stop… *This reporter was shocked to learn that another media outlet is also planning to put out a major story for the upcoming 50th anniversary of Chelmsford Heights, and according to a reliable inside source, "has obtained sensational materials by illegal means in order to serve the higher cause of truth and justice." The reliable source—who doesn't want to be identified because she's not authorized to talk about her paper's crime—confirmed this reporter's suspicions by saying that the ladies of the Chelmsford Heights Women's Alliance "have more skeletons in their closets than are buried in Fiddler's Green Cemetery."*

*So a question of journalistic ethics got posed...*Henryetta tossed and turned. Should she join up with a professional colleague to produce an "exposay"? And maybe win a Pulitzer Prize they would share, or...Her heart took her back to thinking about Billy O'Dell, who she'd been of a mind to let put a leg over tonight... and finally, she fell asleep.

# FOURTEEN

On Monday morning following an uneventful 4th of July, Chester woke up in Shelley's antique French bed, alone. They'd had a "mister-and-missus" on Thursday, another husband-and-wife spat about — what else but a lifestyle addition to the mall — and she'd announced a need for some "away time." It was all his fault she had to leave town for a few days, Chester admitted to himself. He, her husband, was now considered, unanimously this time, the Chelmsford Heights village idiot. He was the cause of the mall's poor sales performance for the first half of the year, everyone agreed, after Mumu Taliaferro declared it to be fact. He was the fall guy for the drastic drop in sales taxes that had shamed Chelmsford Heighsters to admit to municipal "budget considerations" and a forced cancellation of holiday fireworks and festivities.

So no, he didn't blame Shelley for leaving. She, nor he either, could face their friends and neighbors, who had themselves fled the Heights and regrouped at weekend retreats on Grand Lake, while he himself had not left the empty Viceroy Lane/*LeRoi Soleil chateau*. For three days he'd done nothing but worry about how to meet Shelley's lifestyle needs — not even knowing exactly what the term "lifestyle" meant. He felt a desperate need to do something, but…Dad-gum-it! Stumbling out of the wrong side of the bed, Chester stubbed his toe on the freakin' bidet that Bruno Camaleonte had insisted be installed in the "*boudoir d' amour*" for authenticity of lifestyle ambience! What the hell, he was the nominal master of the *chateau*, Shelley wasn't there to stop him, and…Chester felt better than he'd felt in weeks while urinating into Camaleonte's "*toilet d' amour.*"

An hour later, entering the lobby of the mall management office…Oh, no…Chester put a hand to one side of his face and turned to escape, but… "Chester, my man," said Didi "Deal-a-Day" Finegan, the brown-eyed former brunette, former redhead, now blonde real estate broker who had once handled most of the leasing of mall space to tenants. "What on earth has happened to that golden tan you used to wear so well?" she asked. "Have you been sick?" He coughed and croaked yes, but Didi had always been, if nothing else, dogged in her pursuit of making deals, and wouldn't take his claim of raging fever as a no. She practically sat on his lap after following him into his office and starting her pitch for what she called, yet again, the next big thing in retail: "kittens!" she said, "adorable kittens! Everybody loves kittens!"Chester was surprised. Didi had once been kind of a "kitten" herself—"sex sells," she used to say quite persuasively, and she had been, if nothing else, a helluva salesman. But even he knew that pet stores were "so, so yesterday," and though he hated to say so—Didi was only a little older than him and had once been semi-hot—now she herself had become sorta so… so…so…

"Not just a pet store, kiddo," she said, now on her feet, pacing, "no squawking birds, no filthy dogs, none of those creepy-crawly things for creepy-crawly kids, no, no, no—just kittens, kittens, kittens. The store's called 'Kuddlies,' isn't that catchy?"

Chester got up from his chair, refused to sit back down and practically shouted," No! No! No!" to Didi's hard sell. "But Chester, sweet thing," she said, as he headed for the door, "it's the hottest new concept in lifestyle merchandising." Warily, he returned to his chair and listened. "Let's face it, nobody wants to <u>marry</u> a pet of any kind, right Chesty?" she said, with a wink. "We just want to 'fool around' with one for awhile when it's 'fresh' and 'new'—and they don't call 'em 'sex kittens' for nothing, know what I mean?" No, he emphatically assured her, he did not know what she meant and only wanted to know… "What about 'lifestyle,' Didi, what does it mean, how does it work, and what the hell would cats have to do with…?"

"Not cats, honey, kittens," she said, "and therein lies a piece of 'lifestyle tail,' if you'll excuse my little fun-pun. Remember the old Net-Flix concept?" She went on to explain that—like when NetFlix started out in business, sending out DVD's by mail, then taking them back—Kuddlies did the same with felines aged three weeks to three months, after which period adorable kittens became cats that nobody wanted. But first, at Kuddlies stores, customers got to see and touch and bond with their own little darling and take him or her home. "They make great gifts," Didi said. "Research shows that very few girls between the ages of three and thirty-three ever pick up on the switcheroo of look-alike clones sent to them every sixty days. The 'Once There Were Three-Hundred Little Kittens Package' takes them through and beyond that growing-up phase of life. Or for the naturally—let's say the unable-to-decide, fickle types—Kuddlies offers a variety pack of…You'd be surprised by how many breeds, fur patterns and solid colors kittens come in. The company is rolling out a start-up chain of stores immediately, and expects first year sales to top — get this, Chesty — a billion!"

Chester did some rough math in his head. "That's gotta be an awful lot of…felines, Didi," he said. "What does Kuddlies do with the…the used ones when they're sent back?" The veteran real estate broker rolled her brown eyes. "That's what I love about you, Chester, you're so, so…'boyish'," she said. "They…the cats…China! The Chinese absolutely worship cats. They think the awful creatures are vessels of our departed souls, and a good source of protein. So what do you say, hot shot, wanna make a deal?"

"Maybe, but not right now," he answered. "I'd hoped to break ground, or at least announce at the big anniversary blow-out this month, a lifestyle addition to the dead end of the mall, but…"

"Lifestyle addition?! You mean…in bricks and mortar?" Didi said, seemingly with amazement. "What are you going to put in it, Goodwill stores stocked with bell-bottom jeans? I guess you must have missed the memo, Chester: lifestyle shopping centers are deader than disco."

"But you said Kuddlies…"

"Lifestyle shopping centers are dead! Lifestyle merchandising lives on! In upscale malls run by owners not too…too…too busy with other things to know what 'lifestyle' really means."

"But Shelley…her…our…my architect, Bruno Camaleonte… he says…"

"Camaleonte, that fake size-18 con man! He'll say anything to make sale. Chester, my love, your mall already has skylights and 'natural dappled light,' your customers already know when it's a rainy day 'cause the skylights leak. And if you think it's a good idea to try to 're-imagine' a sense of changing seasons in Oklahoma, invest in a couple of new heating and air conditioning units for Rodeo Drive — make 'em feel a nip in the air in late August, a subtle warming in March, hell, buy a big fan and make it as windy in the mall as it is in contrived, open-air, so-called 'lifestyle' shopping centers. All you really need in order to capture the true essence of 'lifestyle' are a few new cutting-edge stores here and there in the mall, each with the right merchandising."

"Yes! Yes! Yes! Didi, you are a lifesaver!" Chester said, rushing to sit on her lap and give the miracle maker a hug. "The Dear John card store space is perfect for Kuddlies! and I can relocate the current tenant overnight! I won't have to commit a felony to win Leo's approval and get his last little acre for Shelley in time for the big anniversary blast!"

# FIFTEEN

Bulldog knew she would always remember this date, July 7th, and not just as the three year, one month, seven day anniversary of her appointment as Chief. No, just as memorable was that it had been the longest, hardest, saddest day of her career. Being an army vet, she'd gone by the book to meet the mayoress' required fifty percent reduction of personnel—forcing her most senior subordinates to take their retirement pensions first, though most were still in their thirties. And tomorrow, as the newly appointed Chief also of the Chelmsford Heights fire department, she would have to repeat the house cleaning process, including also the waste baskets and windows over there. She was happy to pull the extra duty, in part out of gratitude for Mrs. Taliaferro's renewed pledge of loyalty to her. Barring discovery of compelling evidence to the contrary, Her Honoress had said she found it impossible to imagine a slap-and-tickle relationship between Chester Grossman and her, and—even if she were found to be personally liable for wrongful arrest of a shoplifting suspect—her positions as Chief-Chief were secure if no liability for her actions was assessed against the town. Bulldog appreciated that vote of confidence. Though the hour was late, without complaint of fatigue she turned her attention to summarization of the past week's police department blotter: **On July 2:** *Officer on routine patrol noticed suspicious subject in the area of Kent Mews/Rue de Avignon and Viceroy/LeRoy Soleil. Subject advised officer that...*

"Chief Bulldog, sorry to interrupt your important readin'," said a now familiar voice from behind her, "I just thought you might like a biscuit, and came by to show you some old pictures of yourself bein' congratulated, looks like." The chief turned to face the little strawberry blonde reporter for the *Weekly Weekender*... Henryetta, spelled with a "y." It was impossible for her not to like the little brat. Her slightly crooked front tooth and coloration reminded Bulldog of a favorite kitten she'd once had as a pet, and the picture she handed over... "Well, I'll be a monkey's uncle," Bulldog said, looking at a likeness of her Big Behind up in a tree in the mall food court. "And in this one," Henryetta said, "this must be the parakeet you saved from suicide that you're holdin' onto so tight—with Mr. Chester Grossman huggin' you even tighter, by the look of your swelled up face. I'm gonna put it in the special edition, unless..."

"Unless what?" said Bulldog, sensing something foul afoot. "Gimme that!" she commanded, "and all those other ones too." Dad-gum-it it. She now saw that *Weekender* newspaper photos through the years had made it look like she was or had been cozy enough to...to "slap and tickle" with Chester Grossman, who the town was trying to blame for her police actions, and willing to trample over her to do it. And this little Henryetta... Yes, Bulldog sniffed something in the air, the unmistakable aroma of a still warm biscuit. She reached for her cuffs. Trying to bribe an officer of the law with food...On second thought...She waylaid her collar of the little minx sitting there, grinning at her and showing that damned crooked tooth. "Okay, Henryetta," she said, playing it cool with a friendly smile, "what do you want in return for…for your 'favor'?"

"I don't want nothin' 'in <u>return</u>' for nothin'," the little would-be blackmailer said, with an even friendlier grin, playing it even cooler. "But I sure would like to look at the police blotter so I can recollect that popular feature of old *Weekenders* for the special anniversary edition, and I'm gettin' real short of time. Like I said the other night, all our archives got stole."

"Sure, why not," said Bulldog, playing for time. "Let's have a look at the police department's official past blotters." After digging out a bunch of them from a file cabinet, she casually stepped over to her desk and came back with a small recorder hidden in her hand. "'Course you know you shouldn't be looking at those official blotters," she said, as the little snoop continued doing just that. "They're <u>public</u> documents, but you…you pressured me to break the law and let you see 'em, right?"

"It ain't against the law for me to read 'em," the little felon answered, without even looking up to grin. "They <u>are</u> public, and…I didn't want you gettin' in a bother about it, but it would have been against the law for you to keep 'em secret, or alter 'em or somethin' like that. Heck, they've already been put in the paper for everyone to know about."

Hmmm, now that she thought about it, that sounded like something Bulldog had read in a law enforcement manual issued by the state Attorney General, and now that she thought more about it…She started to sweat. "Summarizing, on direct orders from a superior officer, ain't 'altering', not by a long shot," she said, before leaving the little smartass with the blotters and heading for the door.

Hells bells, she'd never wanted to be Chief, not really even a cop, Rosie O'Connor admitted to herself, as she scooted out of the ye olde town hall parking lot on her police motorcycle. She'd only wanted to wear a uniform again, carry a gun and go around visiting with folks, trying to help them get along. And she'd trusted Mrs. Taliaferro, who was, after all…Hells bells, as far as Bulldog knew, the grand dame of Chelmsford Heights had never been actually elected to public office!

Though catching the wind as she sped along Pall Mall Place/St. Trophine, she continued to sweat and…"**APB — public nuisance reported at 6401 Viceroy Lane,**" her shoulder-strapped radio squawked. "**Repeat: APB — public nuisance reported at 6401 Viceroy. Anybody out there?**" The chief radioed confirmation and turned onto Old Gold Boulevard in the direction of Viceroy. She knew what and who the public nuisance would likely turn out to be: old Judge Rice, naked as the day he was born many, many years ago, outside his own wife's bedroom window, peeking between her curtains and…Dad-gum-it! Bulldog hadn't had any call to duty on Viceroy, uh…uh…LeRoy Soleil for quite some time. Many Heightsters didn't want address numbers stuck on their residences. And almost all the houses on Viceroy looked recently re-styled and a lot different than she remembered.

She went back and forth twice before she finally semi-recognized one of them as possibly the Rice chateau, then parked her cycle and scurried to the side of the house. Not seeing any naked old man out and about, Bulldog nevertheless looked in a window and…Shocked by what she saw, she couldn't help herself from blurting into her microphone: "Call Her Honoress! Her daughter is being sexually assaulted…or vice versa!" And the probable victim must have overheard her through the partly open bedroom window. "Please don't call my mother," Phoebe Taliaferro-Dugan wailed. "I was out walking and saw the window open. It's not a crime, my husband's been away for four years. Please…" The probable assailant appeared from under her. "And my wife's been gone for four days!" he cried out. "I thought it was Shelley, crawling back to me through the window." Dog-gone-it! Mrs. Taliaferro, always on alert for such shenanigans of her daughter and granddaughter, would already be on her way to the scene of the crime, it was too late to waylay the call to her.

On the other hand, having reported the incident by only semi-private police band radio, Bulldog reasoned, no one could now say she'd been too cozy with Chester Grossman. On the other other hand, she then realized that wouldn't matter to Mrs. Taliaferro half as much as… A yellow Checker cab screeched to a halt next to her parked motorcycle. "What in tarnation?" said that little *Weekly Weekender* reporter from the driver's seat. "I overheard your radio call at police headquarters and came a-runnin'. Ain't you gonna do somethin' to help out poor Tutu?"

"Nothin' going on here," said the chief. "Mind your own business and go on back to reading those police blotters."

But it was too late.

Dismounting from a Range Rover in her nightgown, Her Honoress was clearly not amused, but for a few moments seemed confused about what direction to charge. At Bulldog for having semi-publicly raised the alarm? At the little *Weekly Weekender* reporter for being there? Or…turning her aim toward Chester Grossman's now darkened house — seized with maternal instinct, no doubt — Mrs. Taliaferro charged across the lawn like a mama rhino responding to a squeal from one of her brood, then began to bang on the door. "Phoebe!" she shouted, "unhand that fool at once!"

"Your Honoress, if I may," said Bulldog, after coming to the mayoress' side with gun unholstered, but before she could… A porch light came on. "How do, How do, How do," said Chester

Grossman, standing in the opened doorway in pajamas, robe and slippers. "Mumu, how nice to see…" Mrs. Taliaferro pushed past him, yelling, "Phoebe, where are you?!" Bulldog followed her toward the first-floor master bedroom, yelling, "Your Honoress, if I may…" But to no avail. The bed was made, the window closed, the curtains drawn. The probable victim was no longer there.

Chief-Chief Bulldog aimed her weapon at the suspect who had followed them to the scene of the crime. "Sorry, Mr. Grossman," she said, "but I'm a straight-shooter, I don't play favorites. What have you done with the body of Mrs. Taliaferro-Dugan, <u>and</u> while we're at it, what have you been doing in truck dock number four?" Aha! The tan man blanched. Bulldog reached for her cuffs. "Welcome to Chelmsford Heights."

She was only doing her duty, but the mayoress put an arm around her shoulders. "Chief O'Connor," she said, "you've been under a lot of stress. It's time for you to take a long, long rest." A camera clicked to preserve the moment. "This'll be a good picture," said the little Henryetta girl, "to go with tonight's *Blotter*."

# SIXTEEN

Though fully aware of the imperious image she projected in the high society of Chelmsford Heights, Mumu Taliaferro thought of herself as warm and down to earth. For example, having read that the practice was common among the olde English upper class, she enjoyed farting when in the company of family and close friends — and otherwise never "put on airs," she would joke, much to the amusement of all. And as mayoress of the town, she was often required to exhibit a cordial absence of distaste for the less fortunate, such as those on the municipal payroll. In genteel circles, however, as she had been taught by her mother's manner before her, she always displayed — in demeanor, appearance and speech — an aristocratic coolness — especially when members of the genteel circle around her smelled blood in the water. In such situations, she made a point to move languidly, smile only faintly, and — even when expressing herself emphatically — to never raise her voice. Mumu Taliaferro literally personified the fashion of large, loose-fitting dresses that made any possibility of her ever sweating absolutely unthinkable to anyone ever in her presence.

So within an hour of last night's brief burst of static on the police radio and her unfortunate encounter with that little hick reporter for the *Weekly Weekender*, she had called for a special meeting of the Women's Alliance, intending to "scoop" the little snoop with her own version of events and chill any spark of gossip before it flared publicly. Fifty or so ladies showed up at her olde English fortress-style home on Kools Lite Lane a/k/a *La Route a la Ruine*—including some members of Shelley Grossman's so-called "French faction," though Shelley herself was reportedly still out of town. Mumu got directly <u>not</u> to the point. "I am terribly concerned," she said to the ladies assembled in her mahogany panelled drawing room, "about this...this girl at the *Weekly Weekender*. Indeed, I fear we have erred in commissioning a special anniversary edition of that newspaper, given that she..."

"Oh no," said someone, "I've told mama and all our out-of-town friends and relatives I'm going to be in *The New York Times* and *USA Today*. We can't, at this late date..."

"The girl seems quite nice to me," said a Mrs. Hardcroft, "very interested in both the Hard and Croft family genealogies, and pretty as a picture. I told my nephew, Robbie, he should call her and..."

"I too have tried kindness toward the poor creature," said Mumu, after raising her hand to cut off meaningless conversation. "Indeed, I offered to provide her with a reference to my personal dentist. But the point is that she has in her possession only some old photos, and"—glancing toward her daughter, Tutu—"she has no knowledge of our affairs, won't take my guidance, and cannot be relied upon to..."

"Oh my gawd," said one of the relatively younger women, looking from Mumu to Tutu, "is she going to put something about last night...you know... in the *Blotter*?"

"No!" said Mumu, practically shouting. She was shocked that any lady of the Alliance, even a new member, would dare to publicly make such a slanderous and tasteless allusion to cheap gossip. The crass *arriviste* would be dealt with later, harshly. "I have already advised Mr. Mixon of our advance displeasure and have cancelled Women's Alliance sponsorship of the special edition," Mumu continued, "so there will be none. I daresay 'Little Miss Mischief' is already no longer among us, and that Mr. Mixon will soon exit Chelmsford Heights as well. Now, let's move on to…"

"But what about the police chief? She knows…"

"Chief O'Connor <u>knows</u> only that her days are numbered," Mumu said, with a freezing glare toward the brash new member that could have iced down a keg of beer. "Ms. O'Connor's obsessive 'attraction' to Chester Grossman has, I fear, unhinged her. She's delusional, her false arrest of an alleged shoplifter at Chester's behest has exposed Chelmsford Heights to tens of millions of dollars of potential liability. Until the case is dealt with, it wouldn't be prudent to dismiss her, but as soon as…"

"And you said Chester's mall is not paying its fair share of sales taxes. What are we going to do?"

"Exactly," Mumu said. "What are we going to do about that hopeless fool, who along with his insufferable social climbing wife is scheduled to co-<u>host</u> the official anniversary celebration?! I fear he too has become unhinged and should be…"

"Oh my gawd, Tutu," said Shelley Grossman, leading a chorus line of high-heeled, leggy Frenchettes into the room. "Are you alright?" she said, going to Tutu and lightly embracing her. "Did Chester make you, you know… 'do it'? Did he try to kill you?" Oblivious to Mumu's glare from across the room that could have fast-frozen a side of beef, Chester's unspeakably tasteless wife turned her attention to the group. "Our first concern must be for poor dear…Is that a moose head on the wall, Mumu? How so… soo…sooo *tres* 'outdoorsy' *chic*," she said, momentarily distracted from her concern about poor dear Tutu. "We need to have a party to raise public awareness of what happened, and provide Tutu with a bodyguard to be with her day and night," she then said. "I know just the man for the job, a Chelmsford Heights policeman, who moonlights as…And those drapes, Mumu, wherever do you find such 'interesting' homespun fabrics?"

To Mumu Taliaferro's amazement and dismay, the jumped-up hussy—whose wobbly social standing in Chelmsford Heights rested solely on Chester Grossman's sagging shoulders—went on to say that Tutu would not be safe from Chester, "you know, 'doing it' to her," if the Women's Lifestyle Alliance did not stand as one to stop him. "I've reported his crazed attraction to Tutu, to the *Weekly Weekender*," she said, "also to *The New York Times*, *USA Today*, and that other local paper, *The Guillotine*. Last night's 'love triangle' with the police chief could have resulted in murder, and ruined the anniversary gala."

As Shelley Grossman went on to enthrall even old guard members of the Women's Alliance with hints of a special appearance by a "Lady Gaga" at the mall affair, Mumu Taliaferro fumed and…Sweating like an air conditioner coil on a hot, humid day—both sputtering and leaking freon gas, as it were—she abruptly declared the meeting adjourned.

# SEVENTEEN

Shelley returned to her home in Chelmsford Heights, having decided not to divorce Chester after all. The process would be unpleasant, the overfed cows of the Women's Alliance old guard, led by Mumu Taliaferro, would again trample her reputation. There would be adverse effects on her social standing, Shelley knew—she'd been through it all before, only a few years ago. Chester had been just as guilty as she of their indiscreet 'doing it' extramaritally, but by the sooo yesterday double standards of the unFrench old guard, she was the one who, for almost a year, felt like she was wearing a so yesterday scarlet letter that clashed with all her outfits. And of course there was the expense of divorce to consider, as well as the distraction from finding a way to make a much needed major lifestyle addition to the mall. So after her appearance at the Women's Lifestyle meeting, she'd called Chester and invited him to meet her in her *boudoir* for an afternoon… A timid knock on the door announced his arrival, exactly on time.

At the appearance of her sooo middle-aged spouse in the open doorway—tanned as a boot from head to foot, drooling—"Let's talk first, darling," she said, with an air kiss in his direction, and like a puppy, off he went, as if to find a place for his bone. Seconds later, back he came—dressed this time, in a robe—carrying a large rolled-up piece of paper in one hand and in the other... "Welcome home, my pet," he said. "I knew I could never put anything over on you, bi-monthly, so here!" Shelley instinctively flinched, as Chester, with a deranged gleam in his eyes, thrust across the French antique desk where she sat—of all stupid things—a stuffed... "Eeek!" she cried, "it's alive!"

"And will be for the next sixty days," he said. "Then I'll send the little rascal to China. But don't be sad, sweetheart, I've ordered three <u>hundred</u> little kittens that will keep you company for many years to come." After he'd again gone to his bathroom, sent there to dispose of <u>his</u> plaything—not anything she would ever have around—Shelley jotted a note on a sheet of her embossed personal stationery. Their *tete a tete* was going to be easier to stage than she'd imagined, she now thought, and... "The Dear John space is a little too big for Kuddlies," her seemingly demented husband announced, coming back at her with his tail wagging, so to speak, "but Didi has another cutting edge client, a Greek guy who's a master French sushi cook—a perfect lifestyle complement." Shelley made another note, as Chester, poor thing, continued to babble. "Chester," she then said, interrupting him, "there's something important we need to talk about. I'm worried..."

"I know, my darling, we need to talk about the mall update," he said, unrolling the sheet of paper he'd put on her desk—a floor plan of the mall, with numerous store spaces outlined in various colors. "Not to worry anymore, my dear. I've figured out how to put lifestyle zing into <u>our</u> so yesterday shopping center, without Leo's cooperation <u>or</u> criminal digging—and without putting dynamite to the mall! 'Lifestyle' is all just a matter of merchandising!" Poor soul, Shelley again thought, as he began to rave about "cutting edge" stores that Didi Finegan—a sooo yesterday real estate broker—was going to fit into the dead end of the mall, as existing leases expired or current tenants were bought out.

Shelley scribbled furiously, as her unhinged husband began to run through various concepts that…some of them were *tres chic*, she had to admit to herself. As a perfect complement to the French food market from California that offered only prepared items, as well as orchids and other lifestyle essentials, for instance, Didi had already made a lease proposal to a hot new restaurant from Portland, Oregon—called "Celsius 40.6"—that offered only meals, uncooked at a specified oven warming temperature in order to preserve the natural flavor and texture of tofu pork chops and other such gourmet dishes. And there were other new concepts like that, on the cutting edge and in keeping with upscale lifestyle. She encouraged Chester to keep talking, as she continued to jot.

"As you know," he eventually said, grinning at her after completing his explanation of the marked-up floor plan, "cutting edge stores cost a lot to get. We may have to bankrupt the mall to put 'em in, but in the longterm…if you're happy and, you know, in the mood to, you know…"

"Chester, I've talked to your father," Shelley said abruptly, "and…" And right on cue, Leo Grossman walked in, looked around with a confused expression on his old face, and… "Oy, in the bedroom already?" he said, before sitting down beside the bed on Bruno's bidet. "Father!" said Chester, opening his arms and starting toward the addled old man, but Leo waved him off. "You're *meshuge*, Chester, like your Uncle Curly, and to boot, a *dumkopt*!"

Shelley stood up and went to her father-in-law's side. "Chester, dear, you've been under a lot of pressure," she said, "and let's face it, you'll be fifty next week, or at least by sometime this year. That's only twenty-five years younger than...Uncle Curly, when he...Your father and I have decided to put you...that it's time you went to the Greener Pastures Home for a long rest. Henry Dugan's out there, you know, and Tutu says he loves it. You two can bury the hatchet, compare notes about, you know, your common experiences with Tutu and, you know, you can do things together like, uh, <u>gardening</u>! Out there, you'll get all the tender loving care you deserve. And not to worry, my love, I promise you I will take care of the mall with the same pride of ownership..."

"Shelley, you sweet thing, always thinking of me," Chester said, now offering his empty open arms to her. "Over my dead body, proud or unproud ownership of the mall you'll be having, *bubbe*," said her surprisingly alert father-in-law, Leo. "When away Chester gets put already, myself I'll be my own trustee."

"But I'm still his wife," Shelley protested. "Evylene divorced him and she got the Fiddler's Green Cemetery to keep for, you know...for being his wife for only a few years."

"So hire Evy's *shmuck* for a lawyer already, try to break the trust again," Leo said. He looked at his still clueless son, then back to her. "A mean junkyard dog of my own I now got already: Morty Wolfe, he goes by, but I call him Hansel!"

"Don' worry, kitten," Chester said, putting an arm around her shoulders after his father had left them. "Didi will..."

"Didi Finegan's a hustler, you idiot," she shouted, breaking away from him. "She's a deal-making addict, who doesn't know squat about lifestyle. <u>Kittens</u>, for cryin' out loud, they're so, so... Cats are the new kittens, and whoever heard of a Greek cooking real French sushi! I promised Brunie—Chesty, we've been making plans—don't you see how much a real lifestyle addition means to me?"

"And dad-gum-it, I'm gonna put one up for you…in stone-and-mortar," her truly insane husband said. "To hell with 'merchandising'! I know, approximately, where the bones Leo wants are buried. I'll find 'em and dig 'em up myself if I have to. Now, c'mon my little kit… cat, your puppy also needs some cud…some scratchin' every sixty days or so."

# EIGHTEEN

Henryetta had got to be pretty friendly with her Peach Street neighbor, Billy O'Dell, since them meeting each other a week ago, though not as friendly as she would have liked. Because of their conflicting work schedules they'd mainly just howdied of a morning and night, with one of 'em goin' to work and the other one comin' home. In the few minutes they's stopped to chat, he'd seemed real interested in her *Weekender* special edition project, and if time had allowed it, she would have asked him about his undertakin' work. So, at the end of the day on Sunday, having just got bad news from her mother, Wynona Sue, Henryetta was cheered up some to see Billy's hearse in his driveway. She parked her yellow Checker, went on over and knocked on his door.

"We were just talking about you," he said. "C'mon in, Henryetta, and meet my mother, Evylene." It was that tall, dark-haired woman—needin' a ride to the airport last week—who was now settin' on the divan. "Do you spell your name with an 'i,' an 'e', or a 'y' like me?" she asked Billy's mother, out of habit. And probably because she was tired, and some upset that her own mama had been kicked off the *S.S. Barge*— put ashore in Panama—and was on her way home with a broken heart.

"You and my mother have a lot in common," Billy said. "She used to be a newspaper reporter, in Frederick, Oklahoma, and now..." He looked at his mama like a little boy askin' if it was okay to... "Now I spell my name with a 'y', my dear," she said, puttin' out a hand, as she changed the subject. "And Mom's also your competition," Billy said, still looking at his mother, but not like he was asking permission for anything. "Evylene owns *The Guillotine*," he then said to Henryetta, "and it's coming out with a special edition next weekend too, an *expose'* about the town of Chelmsford Heights and its people."

Some conversation went on between the three of them, but it was dry as unbuttered toast—not necessarily because Billy's mama was her "competition"—maybe more because Henryetta had decided she didn't want to have anything to do with *The Guillotine* and Clara, the reporter who was puttin' together the "exposay" for Billy's mama. And that low opinion was not just because Clara—probably like the no account ladies of the Women's Alliance—had stole some kind of "materials" for the piece.

Henryetta had got hold of a past edition of *The Guillotine*, a small weekly tabloid like the *Weekly Weekender*—and it too seemed set on promoting certain "lifestyle" notions that she had no use for. While Mr. Harold was forced to put out only "news of the best place and times of our lives" in the paper he bought by mistake, *The Guillotine* motto was *Off With Their Heads!*—printed in a circle around a little picture of the Red Queen from *Alice in Wonderland*—and the paper, admitting it was "counter culture," seemed to be counter about everything else, especially anything having to do with Chelmsford Heights, and men. Under Clara Voinyant's by-line, in a major article, headlined *Heavens to Betsy?NOT!* she'd went on an on about Masons, a men-only secret club in Chelmsford Heights, cremating remains of dead relatives and puttin' the ashes up in jars to change females to males in the hereafter. Henryetta didn't believe a word of it; and had no use for ads in *The Guillotine* either, that were mostly for psychic services, massages, body piercing, tattoos and other nonsense some people seemed to believe in as sources of deep wisdom or displays of being "in on things."

If Billy's mother would have left, Henryetta would have liked to stay awhile. She would have liked to set on the divan with Billy, him with his arm around her shoulders, and tell him…good-bye. She would have liked it a lot if Billy had stayed home from his undertakin' work and kept her company while she felt sorry for herself, and maybe cried a tear or two about this bein' the end of her journalism career and her dream of someday winning one of those Pulitzer Prizes. Instead, she just said she had to go meet Mr. Harold somewhere about somethin', and at the door — after leanin' up to kiss him on the lips — she told Billy O'Dell that by the time he got back from undertakin' in the morning, she'd be gone back to her hometown of Henryetta to be with her mama in her time of sufferin'. Turned out Wynona Sue's gentleman friend wasn't captain of the *S. S. Barge* after all — he was a uniformed waiter — so their marriage at sea wasn't legal. Henryetta felt real bad…for her mother too.

And later, driving over to the suburban town of Bixby to meet Mr. Harold and the wife for supper, she made herself feel worse by composing the last news article she would ever not write: *Mr. Harold Mixon, owner, publisher and editor of the Weekly Weekender, is pleased to announce the resignation of Ms. Henryetta P. Hebert, effective immediately. Miss Hebert's decision to leave the newspaper "for personal reasons" was welcomed by Mr. Mixon, due to the fact that her investigative journalism skills just weren't up to the mark. When a certain suspicious someone kept putting off a meeting with her, Ms. Hebert tried to be as pushy and rude as Katie Couric is with folks on TV. Right after getting a report of a possible assault on Mrs. Taliaferro's daughter, she stuck a bunch of old photographs and a pair of scissors in the certain someone's face — but it didn't work. The prime suspect for theft of Weekly Weekender archives stayed calm as an oyster — just took all the pictures, and the scissors, then drove away in her Range Rover.*

*"Ms. Hebert has been unable to figure out why someone stole twenty-odd years of old newspapers," Mr. Mixon said. "So the special reconstructed edition of the papers for the town's fiftieth anniversary that she's been working on is going to come out just the way a certain suspicious someone wanted it to, without accurate journalism." Though only three days remain to the publication deadline for the piece...*

Henryetta knew somethin' else was wrong, soon as she saw Mr. Harold settin' in a rocking chair on the front porch of the Cracker Barrel restaurant — rockin' back and forth, nervous as a fiddler's elbow. Ordinarily, he only wore his colorful Hawaiian shirt to funerals — to brighten up folks' mood — and when she got up on the porch, he hugged her like she was a grievin' widow her own self. Mrs. Mixon had no appetite and had took to the bed, he said, to explain the wife not bein' there, and he didn't want anything to eat neither. Mr. Harold just picked at his chicken-and-dumplin's platter, hemmin' and hawin' about what bad news he had to tell. She didn't want to burden him with another misery, but after finishing her own catfish platter and a bowl of strawberry short cake, she just blurted out: "Mr. Harold, I hate to tell you this, but my mother..."

"Henryetta, honey, I hate to tell you this," he'd blurted at the same time... "But what about your mother? Not seasick on her honeymoon, I hope." Henryetta bit her lip, to let her boss get back up to telling his news. "These people and their investment portfolios!" he finally said, in the disgusted tone he used when talking about his "Weekender World" customers. "The stock market goes down a tiny fraction, and they do without—they stop going to stores, that then cut down their advertising. These rich people around here, dang 'em, a rain drop falls on the mall roof, sales taxes go down some, and they think the sky is falling. Henryetta, honey, the Women's Lifestyle Alliance…they say they can't pay the balance for the special edition, they've backed out of the project, and…"

"That's nothin to go on about, Mr. Harold. To tell the truth…"

"…you've worked so hard, and done such a good job so far."

"I doubt we woulda won one of those Pulitzer Prizes anyway."

"I know, and I'm sorry, Henryetta, I can't afford to put it in *The New York Times* or the *USA Today*. We'll just have to…"

"Do without…"

"Do without 'em, that's the spirit, Henryetta! 'Cause if I had to give back the money I've already collected for ads, and already spent, I'd have to declare bankruptcy and…I don't think the wife could bare the shame of it all. But more important, much more important, how's your mama liking her honeymoon in…Weren't she and Captain Hornblower bound for Acapulco, Mexico?"

"No, just as far as the Panama Canal," Henryetta felt like she had to say. "And Wynona Sue did get a little sick of the sea, but…She'll get over it, I reckon."

Driving back to Fiddler's Green, Henryetta tried to make herself feel better. Without the ladies of the Women's Alliance, and their money, hangin' over her like a guillotine or somethin', she could crop out some of the bullshit she'd put together for 'em to reinforce their high-britches opinion of theirselves. Clara had scolded her for just pretending to be a journalist, who hadn't even bothered to notice that Chelmsford Heights had no folks "of color" livin' in town, "unless you count 'Mister Tan', that despicable Chester Grossman. And left-handed people too," she said, "they and women with facial hair are treated like trash by Heightsters." The criticism had stung, but now...With or without the archive material, maybe she could write up an exposay just as good as Clara, maybe even better. Heck, maybe *The New York Times* or *USA Today* would pick up the story on their own.

Henryetta felt better—like a gopher finally gettin' into soft dirt—even before she caught sight of Billy O'Dell in her headlights—standin' beside his hearse at the curb out front of her rent house. She parked her Checker in the driveway and went to him. "Get in," he said, "I've got a scoop for you, Henryetta."

He drove to the south side of Fiddler's Green Cemetery, through some old rusted gates and into the moonlit graveyard. Near a big ol' tree, he spread out a tablecloth on the ground, then opened a bottle of cold champagne. "This is how I've been spending my nights," he said, lookin' out on the cemetery grounds—that didn't seem to have any headstones, just a few little flags stuck here and there, maybe to show where graves were still located. "I've been cleaning up the property," Billy said. "If I hadn't been so busy doin' that, I would've been knockin' on your door, and...and askin' you to go out with me to some place nice."

Henryetta reckoned that was Billy's "scoop": news that Fiddler's Green Cemetery was gettin' "cleaned up" to get back in business, and not bein' robbed of bodies to be put up in Mason jars. But she wasn't in the mood for journalism, and let it go at that.

Sharing a single stem glass, they together on the tablecloth, talking at first—mainly about what a trial mamas could be. His mother, Evylene, was just a small town girl from down in Tillman County, Billy said, who'd given up her dream of a career in journalism, and stepped into a lot of bad luck with no account husbands — almost just like her own mother, Wynona Sue, except for the dream part. For years, Evylene had been bitter about it all, according to Billy, again just like her own mother, except that Wynona Sue didn't end up with a lot of money to spend after her divorces, or a son to lean on in her time of need when the money ran out. Billy had come to Fiddler's Green to help his mama get over her hurt feelings about the way she got treated by the people of Chelmsford Heights — which caused Henryetta a little pang of guilt, or maybe it was just the champagne fizz backin' up on her. And now, with his job done, Billy was headin' out at dawn, back to California, where he was raised by his daddy. Billy's dream was to use his recent earnings to buy a metal detector and go back to prospectin' for gold in a town called Venice Beach.

A little before dawn, after they'd gone back to her rent house and had another tumble, Billy O'Dell got up out of her bed. She woke up a few hours later, missin' him some, but found that he had left a long note on the kitchen table, with some sweet sentiments in it, and also…a "scoop of dirt," he called it, that he said he had just as much right to as…his <u>sister</u>, Clara?! Land sakes alive! Billy's farewell note said he hoped the "scoop" might get her journalism career at the *Weekly Weekender* back on track toward someday winning one of those Pulitzer Prizes, and he signed it, "Very truly yours, William O'Dell."

Knowing Wynona Sue wouldn't be up yet after her long plane ride home from the Panama Canal, Henryetta called her and — in the greater cause of truth and justice — left a message on her mother's phone that she would have to suffer on her own for another spell, 'cause the Checker had broke down, and she was gonna be a couple of days late gettin' on the yellow brick road and out of Chelmsford Heights.

# NINETEEN

Walking into Chelmsford Heights Traffic Court on the second level of the ye olde town hall, Willis Willis was wary, but not overly concerned about today's legal proceeding. His client, Mrs. Maude Connolly, hobbling along beside him, had been abruptly called to appear in connection with a delinquent traffic ticket issued to her after she was collared for alleged shoplifting in the Chelmsford Heights Mall. It was no wonder that the old woman, shaken as she must have been by her brutal treatment at the hands of Chief O'Connor, still did not recall having been cited for running a red light on Trolley Street during her alleged flight across the so-called Mason-Dixon Line, so of course she had not paid the fine assessed against her. And in a way, that was a fortuitous failing on her part, Willis now thought, as they sat down on a bench near the front of the court room.

He was not inclined to readily acknowledge any act whatsoever on his client's part prior to her apprehension, certainly no wrongdoing even of a minor nature, and probably could still force a postponement of today's hearing, but on the other hand… The town—known to be scrambling for revenue from every conceivable source to off-set a drop in mall sales taxes—might have exposed itself for an opening barrage of bad publicity by going after its victim, an older woman of modest means—for a two hundred dollar fine plus penalties—in advance of her lawsuit against the town for wrongful arrest. A young strawberry blonde girl in the row in front of him was already jotting notes, Willis noticed. She might be a reporter for the *Weekly Weekender*, he thought. If so, even a likely sugar-coated account by her might serve to get the story into circulation. *The Guillotine*, a radical counter culture rag would pick up on an "injustice of it all" angle, and from there his case might begin to find its way into the mainstream media, and into the heads of Chelmsford Heights leaders.

Chief O' Connor, in full dress uniform—a dead ringer for Rosie O 'Donnell—was in attendance, Willis noted. So was Morty Wolfe, the lawyer defending the town against his lawsuit. And no one else. That a single traffic ticket was the only item on today's docket seemed odd, and…Willis became more wary and quite a bit concerned to see Chester Grossman enter the court room, take the bench, and plop down a desk plaque that identified <u>him</u> as *Traffic Court Judge*. Real and potential conflicts of interest swarmed around the part-time judge's head like flies 'round a fresh cow pie. Willis rose to…He caught a glimpse of Morty Wolfe, faintly smiling, sensed a trap and sat back down. Wolfe's smile faded. Of course, Willis thought, Wolfe had set-up this rinky-dink session, wanting him to object to Grossman's role and in effect concede the merit of a likely town defense that Chief O'Connor was acting solely on behalf of Chester and the mall when she chased down and cuffed Maude Connolly for shoplifting.

"Okay, I think we're all…all know each other, and the facts of the case," the *"Hon. Chester A. Grossman"* said, seeming hurried and distracted by other matters not before him. "The court hereby assesses against the defendant a fine in the amount of…"

"Objection, your Honor," said Willis, on his feet, his jacket now unbuttoned, his pants waist pushed down below his belly. "I'm just a country lawyer, an' while hunerds of dollars may not matter much to folks in Chelmsford Heights, to me and my hard workin', semi-disabled client, Missus Connolly, settin' here—well, we'd like to know what facts she's bein' charged for, same as when she counts out her pennies at the thrift store for used orthopedic shoes and…"

"Okay, okay," Chester said. "Rosie, swear to tell the truth and state the facts of the matter, so we can get this over with." Willis could hardly believe his good luck. At virtually no risk to his real case, it looked like the town might allow him to hear and maybe pre-try its lines of defense in the news media. Chief "Rosie" testified she got an ABP about a suspected shoplifting incident and saw a car… "Objection, Chester," said Morty Wolfe, up on his feet, "this is not a real court, you're not a real judge. This is about a traffic ticket, not alleged shoplifting and wrongful arrest." But Chester, to Willis' amazement, seemed to understand that one line of the town's defense was to throw him to the wolves. He told the chief to go on and tell what happened, which she did, step by step—from seeing Mrs. Connolly's black Honda come out of the mall parking lot, to giving chase through a red light on Trolley Street, to apprehending the shoplifting suspect in the driveway of her residence in Fiddler's Green.

"And what did you do with the shoplifted goods, Miz Chief?" Willis asked, in answer to which Chief O'Connor's face turned red as a rose. "Objection," said Wolfe. "Chester, for cryin' out loud, don't you see the path this so-called 'country lawyer' is leading you down?" Then all hell broke loose, with everybody talking at once about whether there was ever any real evidence of shoplifting. Willis finally quieted the chaos with a shrill whistle. "Well, Judge, I'm just a country lawyer," he said. "I've made mistakes, as I'm sure you know. We both have. I regret 'em, they keep me up at night worryin' about how to make 'em right. And all just because I didn't take the time to think before... Why don't we just get Miz Fanny O'Brien up here an' see if she's missin' anything that mighta got shoplifted."

Again, Wolfe popped up like a champagne cork on New Year's Eve. "Damnit, Chester, this information is part of a more important pending case that, up to <u>now</u> doesn't involve you." But again, Chester ruled against the town's counsel, and in a matter of minutes Ms. Fanny O'Brien, owner of Fanny's Fashion Boutique, had come upstairs and taken the stand, with a bound booklet of papers in her lap. Without being asked a question, seeming to think she'd been summoned by Wolfe, she looked at the dark, thin lawyer and said, "I'm sorry, my inventory doesn't show any merchandise unaccounted for."

"Nothing?! <u>Nothing</u> unaccounted for since the first of the year?!" Wolfe said, practically charging Miss O'Brien. "Gimme that ledger. I grew up in women's undergarments and there's <u>always</u> leakage in panties." He frantically scanned page after page of the store inventory audit. "Aha!" he eventually said, "there's nothing but a red star here to explain what happened to a certain 'Super-Duper Maxi Model Peek-a-Boo panty girdle'! How come? Where did it disappear to? How do you know...?" BANG! "No need to go into all that," said Chester, red-faced through his tan, presumably due to embarrassment about talk of women's intimate apparel. "So," said Wolfe, shaking a finger at the judge, maybe shifting from the town's primary line of defense that a crime of shoplifting had in fact occurred to... "If

Fanny O'Brien suffered no loss," he screamed at Chester, "your tenant wrongfully cried out 'Robbery,' and your Chief of Police and secret lover wrongfully..." BANG! BANG!

"Judge, if I may be heard!" said Chief O'Connor, more colored up in the face—no doubt embarrassed by Wolfe's underhanded reference to the scandalous rumor of her having got caught window peeking on Chester, reportedly because she was jealous in the mistaken belief that he had another woman, not his wife, in his bed—"I can explain the missing evidence, and if I may..." BANG! answered the judge with his gavel. "No need to get into..." But the chief continued, explaining that she'd found the missing Maxi Model girdle only recently, in the mall truck dock number four garbage room, and...BANG! BANG! BANG! "I object!" Judge Grossman himself said, which was strange, as was the sight of Wolfe's public confrontation with the town's Chief of Police. "Where is it? Where has it been? Chief, I demand that you present this so-called evidence here in court!" he said, now apparently feeling committed to his alternative line of defense: that if no shoplifting had occurred, the arrest of Mrs. Connolly had been solely Chester's and Rosie's doing. Chief O'Connor, obviously in distress, testified that the crotchless support garment had been in a police locker or in her personal possession since it's discovery, and then—squirming in her chair, almost in tears—she asked to be excused to go to the ladies room.

Willis could not have been more pleased with himself. He'd lit a fuse, not knowing what would happen, and the town's defense against his lawsuit had virtually gone up in flames. Seeing the little strawberry blonde gal scribbling notes, as Chester and Wolfe continued to fuss, he couldn't help but imagine himself grudgingly portrayed as a brilliant country lawyer in the next *Weekender*. Within days, he would likely receive the Town of

Chelmsford Heights' first settlement offer and the fat lady's song would come to...Chief O'Connor came back into the court room, holding... "What are you trying to pull off here, Miss O'Connor?" Wolfe said to her, snatching the thing from her hands, then sniffing it. "Aha! This undergarment is crotchless but still warm, it's been worn, and recently! You've taken off your own underwear to protect Chester Grossman and yourself against liability for the wrongful arrest of Mrs. Connolly for shoplifting! Don't deny it, Rosie O'Connor, drop your trousers!"

"I didn't arrest anybody for <u>shoplifting</u>," Chief O'Connor said. "I just gave the lady a traffic ticket and told the County Attorney that I suspected..."

"MOTION TO ADJOURN!" Willis bellowed, but it was too late. His case against the Town of Chelmsford Heights and its Chief of Police for wrongful arrest had gone up in smoke. Abandoning his semi-disabled client, Maude Connoly, he retreated from the court room in haste and virtually ran back toward his office.

Dad-gum-it! Those Ivy League law school graduates in the County Attorney's office—there only to get their political careers underway—didn't know c'mere from sic'em about lawyerin'! They'd taken the chief's referral and filed charges without thoroughly...but a lawsuit against the county based on essentially a clerical error would be worth nothing, and...No, dad-gum-it! His own smartass paralegal assistant, Clara, should have vetted the file before he made a jackass of himself and filed a lawsuit against Chelmsford Heights and its police chief, who had rightfully chased and collared a miscreant fleeing a traffic citation! There were identical cases on record and Clara, damn her... "Willis, Mrs. Grossman is in your office," his incompetent assistant announced as he stormed in. "I don't give a rat's ass about that blonde bitch," he shouted. "It's you, Clara…" She put a cautionary finger to her lips, and said, "the other one, Evylene."

Quick on his feet as the trial lawyer he'd been for forty years, Willis "Versus" Willis unzipped his fly, let some spittle drip from the corner of his mouth onto his loosened tie — not wantin' Evylene, his milk cow, to get any notion he was gettin' big city rich off squeezin' her teats. "Well, cut off my horns an' call me an old smoothie," he said, walking into his office. "Ain't it a sight for sore eyes to see…Is that you, Evy?" He'd never before seen a half-Indian gal with platinum blonde hair. "I was thinkin' about you just this mornin', like I always do, and…"

"And in the beauty parlor, I was thinking about you, Willis," Evylene Grossman said. "I was getting made over, for moving back to Chelmsford Heights, where I expect to occupy a position of social prominence, so…I'm sorry, Willis, but I don't think a country lawyer presents a suitable image for representation of my legal and business interests. You're fired. Clara! Have the movers come in to pack up my files. Let's get out of this…this farm building before being seen. I have an appointment at the mall this afternoon."

Willis, stunned by this revolting development and confused about Clara's role in it, zipped up his fly and tried to tidy himself up some. "Now, Evy," he said, "don't let appearances fool you. I've been working in disguise, looking after your legal and business, and <u>personal</u> interests. There's danger out there, Evy," he said, jerking his head toward Clara to signal for her to leave the room while he carried on a confidential attorney-client conversation. But she stayed put, and his client got up to go, so he continued. "Don't dare go to the mall, Evylene," he said, "all your enemies will be gettin' together there in just a few hours for a big anniversary whoop-tee-do and…"

"A whoop tee-do, you say?" Evylene Grossman said. "Sounds like it might be a perfect occasion for me to make my re-appearance. But I'll have to skip the mall gala, I'm afraid. Though I do appreciate your concern and sense of discretion, Willis," she added sarcastically, "which is why I want to have a look at the cemetery property in secret, tonight, in the dim light of the moon. Ha, ha, ha."

"You should be afraid, Evy," Willis said, "you should be very, very afraid. I've discovered, while in my country lawyer disguise, that your ex-husband, Chester Grossman, has hired two thugs known only as Mr. X and Mr. O to...brace yourself...they're planning to kill you!"

"Ha, ha, ha," she laughed. "Chesty would never do that to me. I'm the only woman...Not even his mother ever sort of loved him."

And with that, the best client Willis could ever hope to milk—along with his trusted paralegal, Clara—bolted from the barn.

# TWENTY

Police and Fire Chief Bulldog finished cleaning up the ye olde town hall snack area, and went to the now consolidated police and fire department locker room, to get dressed for tonight's big 50th anniversary blow-out in the mall. At the locker room doorway, she bumped into Mr. X coming out. He was dressed all in black and had charcoaled his face too. "Forgot my miner's headlight helmet," he explained, "got a covert operation on tap." Bulldog hated to interfere with a black op that might lead to a collar of the Marlboro smoker in truck dock number four, but she was shorthanded for tonight's gathering — in one place — of the entire population of Chelmsford Heights, except for kids and pets. "Sorry," she said to Mr. X, "we're out of paper so I wasn't able to post your assignment for tonight. I'm gonna need you to shoot off the fireworks."

"Uh oh," Mr. X said, then for some reason: "are you still cozy with Chester Grossman, Chief?" Dog-gone-it, that cloud over her had been proven to be nothing but smoke. But until the *Weekly Weekender* came out and reported the outcome of today's Traffic Court case, the people of Chelmsford Heights would suspect there had been a spark to their relationship, and that she peeked into Chester Grossman's bedroom because of jealousy. Mrs. Taliaferro had put out that story, Bulldog suspected, after her daughter's missing body was found in her own home, in her own bed—alive and well. Oh well, accusations of window peeking went with being a cop, she supposed, as she began to strip off her work clothes. Law enforcement was a thankless, dirty job—just ask Mr. X—she continued to reflect, but somebody had to do it. If not for a higher call to duty, Mr. X would likely have spent the night, undercover, in the dumpster of truck dock number four. And if not for she herself being needed for the Women's Alliance shindig tonight, Bulldog had no doubt that Mrs. Taliaferro would have already fired her for putting Tutu's name and possibly lost virginity on the air.

She put on her police dress blues, her fire department galoshes and helmet, and Chief badges on either side of her bosom. Ready for double duty, she marched through ye olde town hall and into…Bulldog stopped to take a deep breath of mall air that had been denied to her for five weeks—then coughed. Portable cooking stations lined Rodeo Drive as far as she could see and beyond, as scores of caterers got fired up to assist ladies of the Women's Alliance prepare an elegant meal. Other staff were setting up tables on either side of a red carpet that ran for six hundred feet—all the way to Macy's at the other end of the mall—upon which the ladies would walk the walk of models, showing off the latest lifestyle fashions. All appeared in order, but…

Passing the *Weekly Weekender* storefront, Bulldog detected something not quite kosher, either that or the smell of boiling grease from one of the cooking stations. She found the newspaper's entry door unlocked. Yes, something was definitely afoot inside the *Weekender* office. She unholstered her gun and, warily…In a large room, alone at a table, obviously up to no good, who else would she encounter but the little strawberry blonde reporter from out of town—Henryetta. "What in tarnation!" said the girl, surprised to be caught after mall closing hours mandated for tonight's gala event, but… "Oh," the little sneak then said, "lookee here, Chief Bulldog, I was just now thinkin' about puttin' you on the cover of the official '50th Anniversary Edition' of the *Weekender* that'll be comin' out."

On the table, a piece of cardboard—similar to dozens of others stuck on all four walls of the room—had a photograph pasted on it. The picture in fact showed <u>her</u> astride her police cycle, with the gates at the main entrance to the town behind her. The image blurred, as Bulldog—she couldn't help herself—she shed a tear or two, before pulling the goggles down from her fire chief's helmet. This long overdue recognition was the nicest thing anyone had ever done for her, and made all her hours of selfless duty worthwhile. "You…and the gates, together, sorta sum up my own sorta mixed up impressions of this here town, and—no offense—along with the signs, my mixed up impression of you too, Chief Bulldog," said Henryetta, looking down at the paste-up of the special edition front page, then up to her. "So I reckon that makes you, to me, more symbolic or somethin' than Lord Chelmsford his own self," she said, "even with him settin' over there on a horse in the park."

Chief O'Connor—she couldn't help herself—grabbed Henryetta and hugged her. "I want to apologize to you, Miss Henryetta," she said, "for taking you to be a hardened criminal every time I saw you. Next time we meet, I promise not to put you in cuffs, unless…"

"No need for you to apologize, Miss Rosie," Henryetta said, a little misty-eyed herself, "you were just doin' the best you could under the circumstances and all. I'm not worried none about next time we meet up with one another, 'cause soon as I finish up here tonight, Im gonna get on down the road back to my own hometown that I got named with a 'y' after."

Chief Bulldog shook the girl's hand and turned away. Being hard-nosed on occasions such as this was difficult at times, but somebody had to do it.

# TWENTY-ONE

Oldtime band music drifted in from the big mall party, along with the smell of horse manure and what must have been organically grown onions gettin' fried, Henryetta thought, as she began to review and put final touches to the mocked-up boards for **THE 50th ANNIVERSARY SPECIAL EDITION** of the *Weekly Weekender*—*recalling the best place and times of the lives of the people of Chelmsford Heights.* Satisfied with the front page featuring Chief O'Connor and the town's grand entry gates, she looked at pictures and re-read copy on page 2 related to Mr. Leo's modest erection that got things goin' in a corn field that was now Lord Chelmsford Park. Again satisfied, Henryetta went on to several pages about the mall—that the town had got re-named for, and where an awful lot of its history seemed to have happened. She had a bunch of pictures of unhappy lookin' kids climbing up on Santa's fire engine though the years, and a bunch more of dressed up women lookin' surprised and not so unhappy to be **Caught on the Runway** during mall fashion shows. In fact…

Henryetta now noticed that she had too many of the same… She removed some that weren't of Mrs. Shelley Grossman, who used to be Mrs. Somebody Else, to allow for addition of some goats and pigs to the array of **Proud Pets on Parade**, led by people whose names no one seemed to know. Keeping the Mrs. Grossman photos as limited to there as possible worked pretty good, she thought, 'cause puttin' too many pictures of Mr. Chester's skinny wife next to ones of the old guard of the Women's Alliance—well, to put it kindly—some of those gals would make plenty of shade on a hot summer day. More directly on the subject of ample local appetites, she had put together a whole page on *The World's First Food Court*, with a picture of the statue from the gravesite of Mr. Leo's late wife, Pearl, whose hunger for buttered bagels—in conflict with her clothes shopping—had inspired the original idea of putting all the mall's fast food together on a second level section of Rodeo Drive.

Henryetta next scanned old pictures of Chelmsford Heights women standing in front of stores—that must have been for ads—and reckoned they might take some readers down memory lane, 'cause all the stores seemed to have gone out of business in the mall since then. She'd heard of only a few of the bunch that included J.C. Penney, Bonwit Teller, Sharper Image, Harold's, Connolly's, Laura Ashley, Bailey Banks & Biddle, F.A.O Schwarz, Nature Company, Smith & Hawken and Walden Books. Same for some restaurants—The Magic Pan, Houlihan's, Steak & Ale, TGI Friday and Sfuzzi. It was a sorta forlorn section, to Henryetta, sorta like the double page spread…She was still undecided about her hurried, last-minute reconstruction of the old **Where Are They Now** features that seemed to have been so popular. Headstone after headstone shown standin' in Fiddler's Green Cemetery—inscribed "Here Lies Uncle Bill," or "May

So-and-So Rest in Peace," or... "Charlie Parker the Weekly Weekender Man"?!

Dang it! According to Mr. Harold's suspicious mind, Mrs. Taliaferro had intended to scare him by seeming pleased that Mr. Parker's dead body had been found in Fiddler's Green Cemetery a few weeks ago after — Mr. Harold thought — him bein' recently killed, or somethin'; but accordin' to his gravestone he'd been planted there more than ten years ago! Maybe she'd been wrong about the Grand Dame of the Women's Lifestyle Alliance bein' behind the theft of the *Weekender* archives, Henryetta now had to admit. That thought made the dreary subject of passed-on folks even more depressing to her, and toward the end she'd still had to put in some pictures and words about the town's new Call-'n-Bury-'Em — spelled ***C-o-l-u-m-b-a-r-i-u-m*** in olde Italian Latin or somethin'. Next to a picture of the sealed niches for Mason jars of ashes, in an open slot, just for fun — and to sorta recognize Mr. Moe Goldberg's previously unknown contribution to the naming of the mall and town — she'd inserted a photo of an old Chelmsford Jam jar she found online.

Maybe she should include a second picture of Mrs. Pearl Grossman's more unusual and eye catching statuary gravestone to liven up the ***Where Are They Now*** section, she thought, searching for a copy in a stack of discarded photographs. Mr. Chester had got sorta sentimental lookin' at it, she remembered. "Mother," he'd said, pickin' it up and holdin' it to his heart. Not able to see what he was seeing from across his desk, she'd asked if it was a good likeness of his mama that he'd like her to include in the special edition, and...Dang, she must have left the extra picture in his mall management office.

On a more upbeat note, she had dozens of party pics on the boards, showing the dressed-up folks of Chelmsford Heights havin' real good times of their lives at dinner dances at the country club and such, and just casually eating and drinking at bruncheons and bar b-qs and the like. The affairs were all for worthy causes, not just for frivolous fun, Henryetta had been told, and she could see that was true fact from banners in the background of some of 'em. Lord o' mercy, it was no wonder Chelmsford Heights was such a fine place to live, what with all the good works of the ladies goin' on all the time. Awards ceremonies for good deeds looked like full time jobs their own selves for a lot of women in the town...or maybe not so many, she noticed. Seemed like the same gals handing plaques back and forth to one another, now that she looked at the bunch together. She knew she'd gotten the names of Tutu Taliaferro and Shelley Grossman right, but now she couldn't be sure which was handin' out a plaque and who was receivin' one. Movin' her head back and forth between separate photographs of 'em, it looked almost like they'd been tuggin' back and forth from year to year over the "Woman of All Time Award for Outstanding Achievement in Personal Hygiene," or somethin'.

Oh well, time was short for the printers to pick up the boards, so Henryetta moved on to several layouts: **Perfect Kid of the Weekend, Perfect Pet of the Weekend, New Chateau of the Weekend, Greenest Lawn, Prettiest Garden, Newest Kitchen, Cutest Couple** and so on. Then there were all the statues around town to show, including the one of Lord Chelmsford of course, to which...Henryetta had to move closer and squint her eyes to make out the photoshopped print of the Lord's pedestal inscription that—to make clearer—she had sorta semi-accidentally "botched": **Learn nothing from [this place] except how not to behave.** And speakin' of "lordy"! the **Chelmsford Heights Hall of Fame** section would have been thick as a Tulsa phonebook if she hadn't used small pictures and tiny print, and would have been about as useful since almost all its members were still alive and still local residents, as far as she could tell.

And finally, Henryetta came to the *Police Blotter* features.

In the party pictures there had been a lot of changing of Misters-and-Missuses at social affairs through the years. And for awhile Henryetta had thought one or more of those do-si-dos of bedmates—all of 'em involving scandalous hanky panky, according to her 4th of July conversation with Billy O'Dell's sister, Clara—might hold the secret of why the Women's Alliance had stole the *Weekender* archives. But later—divorces were so dern common in Chelmsford Heights, as well as bein' matters of public knowledge—she had abandoned that notion and put all her focus on gettin' hold of whatever had been published in the *Blotter* that the ladies might've been so het up to stifle. There was so much dirty laundry in those records that Chief Bulldog finally let her look at, she was surprised that the prior *Weekender* owner—and more surprised that Mr. Harold too—ever published 'em, and danged surprised that Mrs Taliaferro and others hadn't threw a hissy fit about it.

'Cause the police department blotter showed there was just as much over drinkin' and throwin' dishes and everyday and night misbehavin' in the history of Chelmsford Heights as there was in her redneck hometown of Henryetta, Oklahoma, maybe more. And at one time or another—not just Tutu Taliaferro out walking so often in Chester Grossman's neighborhood—one member or another of every prominent family in town seemed to have brought shame and embarrassment on theirselves and others—just like her own mother, Wynona Sue, who took up with the daddy of her high school boyfriend, Gaylord Goodhart, and got arrested for bein' shit-faced drunk and bare-assed necked in a wrecked school bus that wasn't s'posed to be drove off school property and…Henryetta fanned herself with a left-over photo as she walked over to a water cooler to calm herself down some. The mall party was gettin' goin', she could tell from the louder, livelier music she heard, along with some men hollerin' "Take it off, Shelley!"…then, "Put it back on, Tutu!"

From a distance at the rear of the room, Henryetta looked back at the mocked-up boards. She couldn't help but laugh out loud at the spread on **Lord Chelmsford's Balls**, even though the joke might have been on her, she reckoned. She hadn't even known what the pictures of young gals in fancy dresses and sashes were about, and had never heard of the term "debutante" 'til she looked it up online. After reading that the original purpose of such balls back in olde England was for members of the upper class to introduce their virgin gals to polite society—eligible bachelors, to be plain about it—she still couldn't help but think of pictures she'd seen of the famous Fort Worth Fat Stock Show. And in Chelmsford Heights for the past twenty-odd years, she reckoned that most of the debs had already been "introduced" to boys, and then some, before gettin' "presented" at their "coming out" balls. Probably she was just jealous, she thought, 'cause she never had a daddy to throw a party for her and stand up next to her so proud and…

And now Henryetta noticed that there were no pictures of the men of Chelmsford Heights on the boards doin' anything <u>but</u> standin' or settin' next to women, usually at a party of some kind, with a glass in hand. As far as she'd been able to see, all the husbands, except for Mr. Chester, drove off to Tulsa every morning to practice bein' lawyers and doctors and accountants and such, then came drivin' back through the town's opened ornamental gates at the end of the work day. On weekends, they sorta hid out at the country club, it seemed, in areas where women weren't allowed—playing games with one another or, according to Clara and *The Guillotine*, hatching "Mason's plots against women." Henryetta herself just couldn't see how the gals of Chelmsford Heights were so put upon, as Clara claimed. To her, it seemed like the ladies ruled the roost in town, but...Henryetta put aside a passing notion that it might have been Clara who stole the *Weekender* archives, not to dig up dirt necessarily, but maybe to keep her, *The Guillotine's* competition, from writing anything good about the well-to-do folks on this side of Trolley Street. Clara admitted she stole some "materials," but...

Henryetta looked at her watch and walked back over to the **Police Blotter** board, again wondering what the Women's Alliance—or more particularly, Mrs. Taliaferro—might have been so desperate to keep out of the official town history and—the Great Dame thought at the time of the archives theft—out of *The New* York Times or *USA Today*. Mumu shouldn't have worried none, she now thought, her exposay wasn't gonna get published in either of those out-of-town newspapers without the Women's Alliance payin' an ad fee for it. And everybody in town must have still remembered from only four years ago that the "Masked Pollinator" who deflowered a bunch of gardens in Chelmsford Heights had turned out to be TuTu Taliaferro's husband, Dr. Henry Dugan, who seemed to have just disappeared afterward. So she her own self had fell plum flat as a gander's arch, Henryetta thought, and had nothin' worth nothin' to show for her three weeks of investigating theft of the past *Weekenders*.

As she turned to her work table, it occurred to Henryetta that whoever stole the archives might not have had nothin' to hide at all, but instead might've been tryin' to find something his or her own self. And maybe it was all for the best, 'cause the theft had given her—and maybe the Heightsters their own selves—a chance to re-remember their past and maybe shake off some of the crust that had built up through the years. With that thought and a last unclassified photo in hand, Henryetta returned to the final board of pictures and captions titled *Lest We Forget, They Also Served*, showing longtime local store keepers, waiters, nannies, maids and butlers and such. Mr. Harold hadn't published the picture of Kuku Taliaferro with her hand down in Chef Gregory's pants, but her boss had gone to an important business meeting at dinner, and left the final edit of the 50th anniversary special edition up to her.

After the newspaper printer came by and picked up the boards, Henryetta turned off the lights. Not wantin' to intrude into the big mall party—gettin' rowdier by the minute to judge from all the hollerin'—she went out the back door into a service corridor and…She saw light coming from an open doorway down the hall and heard Willie Nelson wailin'. Even though her Checker was loaded up and she needed to get on down the road, Henryetta was curious, and walked on down the service passage that served the *Weekly Weekender* office, a chiropractor clinic and Mr. Leo's unusual place of residence. She'd intended to say good-bye to the likable old man, but…

Land sakes alive! A storage room was pert near filled to the ceiling with cardboard boxes… and stacks of the missing old *Weekenders*!

Tacked all over a large wall, someone had stuck up a bunch of cut-out "Where Are They Now" photographs, and connected the tacks together with different colored strands of knittin' yarn that…It wasn't rocket science, but the strings of yarn all came together to pinpoint a picture of the statue marking Pearl

Grossman's grave in the Fiddler's Green Cemetery, not far from a big Sycamore tree Henryetta had noticed in some of the other graveyard photos. It was the same shot Chester Grossman had been so moved by when he saw the original, and… "Well roll me up and smoke me!" Henryetta muttered to herself. Stuck on one side of the wall with a claw-like gardening tool, a scrawled note: *D DAY JULY 22!*—that was tomorrow—and leaning on the wall…Mr. Leo's shovel from his Last Little Acre!

"D" was for "Dig Day"! Mr. Leo had took the archives to find the location of his late wife's gravesite that he must have forgot.

Though he had committed a crime, and put her to considerable trouble, Henryetta almost came to tears to see such evidence of a forgetful old man's remembered affection for a woman named Pearl, *aloha ha-sholem.*

# TWENTY-TWO

In black tie and blackface, Chester Grossman—hiding behind a tree trunk on the perimeter of the Chelmsford Heights Mall parking lot at the Macy's end—gave up on his accomplice, Mr. X, and decided to undertake on his own the covert operation they'd planned. Dragging a shovel, carrying a backpack of other supplies—including a stick of dynamite—he crawled fifty yards or so to the Chelmsford Heights side of a sewer recently installed beneath Trolley Street, and…Geronimo! Into the darkness of the sewer he went. Chester was hell-bent, a man possessed with rescuing the remains of his late mother from the bowels of Fiddler's Green Cemetery, where "Evilene" held them in her surly grasp. His life, or at least his happy marriage to Shelley hung in the balance. Only by winning his father's forgiveness and gratitude would he be able to give his wife the lifestyle addition to the mall she yearned for.

The statue of Venus de Milo that had marked his mother's grave—Evylene had sent it not only to mock him, Chester had come to understand, but also to make it impossible for him to locate where "the pearl more valuable than all the riches of his tribe" was buried, or so the conniving wench had thought.

With the aid of an old *Weekly Weekender* photograph, however, showing the gravesite statue where it had stood, not far from a large Sycamore—and with some expensive assistance from NASA—Mr. X was fairly sure he had found the buried treasure, encased, unfortunately, in an underground concrete-lined crypt.

So, this being the only night for weeks that Mr. X had not committed to one of his hobbies, Chester had excused himself from the head table of the 50th anniversary mall gala, and hoped to get back and cleaned up in time to make a dramatic announcement of his coup at the evening's climax. But… "Dad-gum-it!" he'd hit a dirt wall. Excavation for the sewer connection into Fiddler's Green seemed to be not yet completed.

Not to be denied, Chester began to burrow.

"Yes, there's quite a shindig going on inside our mall," Chief-Chief O'Connor said into the camera of a Tulsa television station that had sent a crew to cover the affair. "My job is to secure the perimeter, and at the stroke of midnight set off a barrage of…"

"Exactly what are the citizens of the town protesting against?" asked the blonde TV reporter, holding a microphone. "The alert we got from *The Guillotine* wasn't clear about…"

"Chelmsford Heightsters haven't got anything to protest against," said Bulldog, "that cheering you hear from inside the mall is for themselves, and fifty years of proud upscale lifestyle, liberty and pursuit of…" Unable to hear her own self talk, Bulldog turned to quiet the loud racket from behind… "Over our dead bodies! **Over our dead bodies! OVER OUR DEAD BODIES!**"

came the chants of a rabble crossing Trolley Street, hundreds of old hippies, Bulldog estimated, carrying printed placards demanding *JUSTICE FOR BIRDS NOT BIRDIES!* and *OFF WITH THEIR HEADS!* and *DOWN WITH MASONS!* Bulldog detected anarchy afoot!

"A nozzle! Bring me a nozzle!" the Chief-Chief commanded, but dad-gum-it, the fire hose finally brought to her by one of the TV crew seemed to be not connected to anything at the other end. Without time to issue a reprimand to any subordinate, for she could find none, Bulldog ran the length of the empty flat hose, hooked it to a hydrant, and with her bare hands turned on the water to full force. Instantly, the hose swelled up and began to writhe and thrash about like an enraged python, spewing a barrage of liquid cannon fire, thankfully, in the general direction of the invading forces from Fiddler's Green.

Bulldog struggled to subdue the beast, finally got a hammer-lock hold on its head, then mounted a full-scale counter-attack against the protesters with well aimed release of a virtual tsunami that washed the mob—and regrettably, the blonde TV reporter—back across the Mason-Dixon Line and into the gutter of Trolley Street in front of the Chew-n-Choke truck stop cafe. Finishing off the enemy, spraying left and... "Uh oh," said Bulldog, at the sight of Pop Barnett's black-and-white police vehicle toppling off its blocks and into a newly excavated ditch.

Inside the mall, meanwhile, Mumu Taliaferro was not amused. Standing <u>on</u> the head table at center court, she looked toward the Flying Flamingos Court, then toward the Prancing Peacocks

Court, trying to catch sight of Chester Grossman through greasy smoke that filled the air. She had numerous complaints to vent. Unruly men and, alas, so-called ladies, were throwing inedible so-called food at each other from table to table. Chef Gregory's newly recruited auxiliary staff of unversed waiters continued to re-fill wine glasses with cheap grain alcohol that the mall merchants association had provided. The heat—to judge by the sweat pouring into her *decolletage*, the mall temperature must have been at least a hundred degrees, Mumu imagined. And now…to her astonishment and dismay, dozens of kittens seemed have wandered in, no doubt drawn like flies to a pervasive smell of rotting fish that seemed to be coming from a store space with a new-looking sign— *Army Surplus Sushi From France.*

Waiters and guests swatted at the disgusting baby cats with their shoes, cursing like drunk sailors, but there must have been at least three-hundred of them and… "Oh dear, who could be so cruel to pussy cats?!" said her daughter, Tutu, from her left. "So who told you my name was Katz already?" said Leo Grossman from her right.

No, Mumu Taliaferro was definitely <u>not</u> amused. The planned climax of the town's glorious 50th anniversary celebration was a complete disaster, it was all Chester Grossman's fault, and she desperately wanted to show her displeasure to the fool's face. To please that *nouveau riche* hussy of a wife, who continued to strut up and down the runway in increasingly skimpy outfits—like Salome, for heaven's sake, calling for John-the-Baptist's head on a platter—Chester had brought disgrace upon Chelmsford Heights. And his highly improper advances toward her foolish daughter, Tutu, after spurning her hand… "Oy," said Leo Grossman, lifting the hem of her long skirt from behind and below her, "with *tuchuses* like those already..." Tasteless! this entire affair was utterly tasteless!

Across the invisible line under Trolley Street, having been aided by a mysterious surge of water from the sewer, Chester poked his head out of the ground into moonlight and checked his position by the GPS gadget he'd bought at the online NASA gift shoppe. Yes, he had arrived in the prime corner section of the Fiddler's Green Cemetery once favored by Chelmsford Heightsters, he concluded. Just as Mr. X had reported, the area had been cleared of headstones, but not, he prayed, of all bodily remains of...He shook his head to get dirt out of his eyes, then shook it again. He'd drunk too much of that godawful wine at the party and must be hallucinating, he thought. Crawling on the course indicated by the GPS gadget, he neared... "Oh my god!" The statue of Venus de Milo <u>was</u> back in place!

That wicked witch, Evylene, must have...No, the figure moved! A tall angel with platinum halo—come to steal his prize—walked toward him, holding erect the body of his dear departed...Clara O'Dell? No, the mysterious figure was not an angel, and not an hallucinatory figment of his tortured mind, but a...a...platinum blonde-haired demon succubus that resembled...Aghast with horror, Chester recognized the grave robber silhouetted against a rising moon as...EVILENE!

Again meanwhile, Chief-Chief O'Connor, in her latter capacity as head of the fire department, assumed responsibility for the fireworks display after finding that her subordinate on loan from the police department, Mister X, must have taken a coffee break from duty. All the Roman candles, exploding rockets and other packaged ammo seemed in order, she saw from the light of a fiery flare she carried. At exactly the stroke of midnight she would... Uh oh, in her other Chief capacity, wearing a different helmet, so to speak, she noticed that a high-intensity arc light—that should have been pointed toward the sky to create the aura of an important event, such as a movie premier—had tilted in the direction of a mall wall, and...In the light she detected cigarette smoke coming—not from truck dock number four, but from truck dock number <u>three</u>! In hot pursuit, she set out to nab the incorrigible smoker in the act and snuff out the spreading menace of tobacco use in Chelmsford Heights.

Huffing and puffing, she got to the crime scene just in time to see... "Chief-Chief, it's you," said Mister X, grinding his foot into the ground in obvious frustration. "Looks like we just missed our perp, and check out these butts. It's the Marlboro man at it again, just as you suspected."

BOOM!

Bulldog, thinking the flare she'd dropped behind her must have set off the fireworks, looked at her watch. Ten o'clock. Close enough by military standards, she decided, but...huffing and puffing back to cover up her two-hour error, Bulldog detected flames and smoke rising from Fiddler's Green Cemetery. And with the flare back in hand, she then saw that the fireworks were all still accounted for. Again she looked at her watch. Oh well, she was a short-timer and getting hungry for a snack, so Bulldog hurried along the rows of shell tubes, lighting fuse after fuse after fuse after... "Uh oh." Either the gun powder had gotten damp or someone had miscalibrated the trajectories of the *Big Bada Boom* ammo packages, she realized, as Roman candles, exploding rockets and other 4th of July warheads rained down on the roof of the mall.

Bulldog again ran to the fire hose, subdued its wild writhing again, and commenced watering in the direction of the mall's center court where the town brass were headquartered, but... Dad-gum-it! Due to problems of distance and maybe waning water pressure, her barrage fell short and hit the panicked mob of partygoers fleeing though the center court doors, forcing them back into the burning building. And...

And here came the Fiddler's Green protesters again, sopping wet but chanting even louder than before: **JUSTICE FOR THE BIRDS! JUSTICE FOR THE BIRDS! JUSTICE FOR THE BIRDS!**

After looking up at the sounds of fireworks that couldn't even be seen through mall skylights as Chester had promised, Mumu Taliaferro returned to reading her speech for acceptance of another lifetime achievement award from the Women's Lifestyle Alliance. But then, in reaction to rude catcalls of **OFF WITH**

**HER HEAD! OFF WITH HER HEAD!** she again looked up, sensing yet something else amiss.

Mumu was absolutely appalled by both what she saw and couldn't see. Smoke from the French faction's idiotic home cooking stands had thickened. Indeed, flames of Shelley Grossman's organic prairie oyster kabobs—tended to by Chef Gregory at last notice—looked almost out of control. And to judge by the now weakening chants of "Off With Her Head," her audience seemed to be rudely leaving—except for Tutu of course, seated beside her, and Leo Grossman on her other side, who seemed to have rudely nodded off.

Yet again, the fault lay at the feet of…Mumu and Tutu dropped their jaws in shocked unison. Chester Grossman, finally, staggered through the smoky chaos—a ghastly sight to see in blackened face, tattered muddy clothes, and in his eyes—the deranged gleam of a maniac—holding out a gunny sack stuffed with… "Father!" he shouted, waking Leo Grossman. "It's mother, there was an explosion and a fire, but I scooped up her ashes with other cremated debris from her coffin. Now, c'mon you lovable old codger, you, give your son a hug."

"And me too, Chesty!" cried Tutu, climbing across the table. "I'm lovable too, I'll give you a hug."

"*DUMKOPT!*" the old man roared. "Such a *dumkopt* already! Gold certificates! Tens of millions of dollars in gold certificates I buried to keep from the tax man! So a hug I should give already to a son who turns my fortune into ashes?! Oy, such a *dumkopt*."

# THE
# END

# EPILOGUE

**From Where I Sit…..An Editorial Opinion by Harold Mixon**
These will be my last words published in the *Weekly Weekender*, and I'm sure we're all glad of it. I have sold this newspaper that serves the good people of this area to Ms. Evylene Grossman, a former resident of Chelmsford Heights, who will soon move back to town to rejoin her many old friends. As reported on this week's front page—a scoop by our dogged investigative reporter, Henryetta P. Hebert—Ms. Grossman, owner of Fiddler's Green Cemetery, has completed clearing a portion of the property for development of a major so-called "lifestyle shopping center" to be called Mason-Dixon Promenade. In the future, the *Weekender*, under the management of her daughter, Clara, will be operated mainly to connect the stores and restaurants of the new facility and their Weekender World customers—essentially as a kind of weekly reciprocal infomercial, with lots of party pictures and ads.

Which brings me to the subject of this weekend's *50th Anniversary Special Edition, recalling the best place and times in the lives of the people of Chelmsford Heights* —also produced by Miss Henryetta. With the fiery destruction of the mall between Macy's and Ye Olde Town Hall, where so much of local history has been centered, the special edition insert may be especially treasured by some. It should be, for it shows this town and its people in the best light possible, much to Henryetta's credit as a journalist. Many of you have been unkind to her—you know who <u>yew</u> are—and no doubt a photo outline left blank on the last page means to tell you she could have responded in kind with an exposé of various things about your behavior not to your credit. Instead—at great danger to herself that I dare not discuss publicly even now—she put together a collection of photographs and captions documenting your history and lifestyle as, in her words, "a big ol' fifty-year fashion show."

Her work shows numerous such ingenuous insights of a small town girl—including the front page picture of Police Chief O'Connor with the Chelmsford Heights ornamental gates closed in the background, photoshopped to place the chief <u>inside</u>, seemingly to guard against the town's citizens <u>exiting</u> into the world around them. She treats many of the less admirable qualities of "Heightsters" as understandable and forgivable foibles of human behavior—such as cliquishness on children's playgrounds to country clubs as amounting to about the same tribal thing, writ large, as commendable state pride and self-congratulatory patriotic nationalism. And as for your slavishness to rules of fashion, well, as she points out, except by changing from cottons to tweeds after Labor Day, despite ongoing 110 degree Oklahoma weather, there would be hardly any sense of autumn in Chelmsford Heights at all. A common expression of Henryetta's, about almost everyone is, "I reckon they're doin' the best they can under the circumstances and all." She laughed at others and their ways, it's true, but first and last Henryetta laughed at herself. If they handed out Pulitzer Prizes for this kind of piece, I'd say she would deserve one.

It got me to re-thinking some things. Preoccupation of some folks around here with "lifestyle"—both adjective and noun—is not so different than the pioneering notions of our forefathers and foremothers who we so rightly admire so much. Pride and pleasure in, say, a fancy old chifferobe or chandelier—gaudy and out of place in a sod house as lipstick on a pig—made life more tolerable for some out here in the early days on the prairie, especially the ladies. They had to "make up" a more genteel way of life out of just about nothing. And when Okies got to making some money and importing uppity notions for decor and debutante balls and such from the so-called upper classes back east, they were doing nothing but what those so-called elites did in modeling their lifestyles after that of Olde European upper crust—nothing except maybe <u>not</u> pretending they weren't proud as Aunt Pat's meringue pies about what they'd achieved by their own hard work and good fortune. What is "lifestyle," after all, but "civilization" writ small?

Anyway, Henryetta's gone back home, and the wife and I will be following her in the next day or so. I won't live to see it, but I can't help wondering what she would find if she came back up here in another fifty years. I doubt the mall will be re-built, what with both Mr. Grossmans having run off—Mr. Leo reportedly to Rio to protect expected insurance proceeds from taxation, and Mr. Chester reportedly to Mexico with Mrs. Tutu Taliaferro-Dugan—and with Ms. Evelyn Grossman putting up the major shopping center <u>and</u> a bridge across Trolley Street to connect to Macy's. Not just any ol' bridge, but an exact copy of Venice's famous Ponte Vecchio, lined with exciting new "today stores," such as one called "Kuddlies" and another selling biodegradable yogawear, according to noted architect, Bruno Camaleonte and his new fiancee, local broker, Didi Finegan.

To accommodate Ms. Grossman's generous return of all the remaining remains of so many former residents of Chelmsford Heights, as well as meet future municipal needs, maybe the former mall site should be "re-imagined" as…well, you know everybody's gotta go sometime. Signs saying "Welcome" and "Residents Only" would fit nicely with a gated entrance to a new cemetery, and as Henryetta might say if she were to see such a sight — "nothing worldly much matters at the end of things, I reckon."

www.ingramcontent.com/pod-product-compliance
Lightning Source LLC
Chambersburg PA
CBHW050941120626
46552CB00001B/320